Coming Together
In Vein

Lisabet Sarai

editor

Coming Together: In Vein

A Coming Together Publication
EroticAnthology.com

TO OUR READERS,
WHO HELP US MAKE A DIFFERENCE

Table of Contents

Lisabet Sarai, editor

Introduction

Not another vampire book....

I'm afraid so.

You may believe the world already holds more than enough stories about seductive, sparkly blood suckers. Fear not (or perhaps a bit of fear *is* appropriate); the vampires you'll find in these pages will surprise you. From C. Sanchez-Garcia's Nixie, cursing in German and teasing the lover who frees her from the need for blood, to Nobilis Reed's nano-engineered corporate gore-guzzler, the authors who have generously shared their creativity in this volume take the stereotypes and tear them to bloody shreds.

Why vampires? you might still inquire. For a long time I've wanted to publish a Coming Together book to benefit Doctors Without Borders (Médecins Sans Frontières or MSF), an organization that provides urgent medical aid to those who need it most, regardless of their race, religion or political affiliation. Right now, as I write this introduction, MSF is assisting the victims of civil wars in Syria, Sudan, and the Democratic Republic of Congo; helping street children in Honduras; working to contain a cholera epidemic in West Africa; battling measles in Somalia and malaria in Niger. Just a few weeks ago, MSF personnel were in New York and New Jersey, helping fill the medical needs of Hurricane Sandy victims. The brave MSF doctors and nurses in the field often face daily violence and government persecution, in addition to horrific conditions of sanitation and persistent shortages of essential supplies. I'm personally awed by their dedication to service.

Despite the current abundance of vampiric fiction, all evidence suggests that readers' hunger for stories of the undead remains unsated. I decided to put together a vampire book because, quite simply, I thought it would sell - and the more copies we sell, the more money we make for MSF.

I'm hoping readers will be willing to bleed a bit, for such a great cause.

Of course, the tales in this collection aren't just vampire stories. They're vampire erotica. I guarantee they'll make you shiver, from terror, desire, or both. Our vamps are sexier than the Twilight crowd - and a lot more original.

Enjoy!

Lisabet Sarai
December 2012

Nixie's in Love

© C. Sanchez-Garcia

"*Shiesse*—you're so negative, you don't like any of my ideas." Her English was good, but for cussing or passion she preferred her native German.

"It's just a bad idea. You seem like an alcoholic circling the bottle some nights. You keep thinking about this stuff and I'm worried you're going to go back..."

"You're worried I'm crazy, *jah*? Say it, why don't you?"

Daniel waved his hands. He didn't want to say it. It was stupid to let himself get drawn into another argument. "You're so close to beating this thing, I don't want to see you go back. That's all, *nordchen*. You need to stop. We have to trust each other."

Sitting with her bare feet up in her beanbag chair on the other side of the room, Nixie looked down, vacantly examining her toes. She shook her head and her bright mane of silver-blonde hair covered her small, squarish face. She was sulking already and the night was still early.

Next to the kitchen door the wall clock, which they'd bought together at the Dollar General store, made small dinging noises and stuttered as if reproaching them. The doorframe next to it was cracked from the weekend before. Near the number five where the little hand was half dangling, a large triangle of clear plastic was missing. Behind the loose hands was an image of Jesus of the Sacred Heart in circus-poster colors. She said she liked to look at it, because it reminded her of the stained glass windows in the little church in Oberammergau from long ago when she was a young girl.

"What about pirates?"

"Pirates?" said Dan.

1

She brightened and sat up straight, dropping her feet to the floor. "They have these Somali pirates, you know? In the Africa? Do you hear them on the news programs? There are these pirates, you see this, and they come out late at night, this is perfect, listen. They come out at night when they rob the ships, and we are on the ship, maybe I am in a trunk or a box—like in the movies, you know? Like that one 'Nosferatu' where the Dracula, he travels in this box, see, in the ship but then at night he comes out like this." She raised her arms and tensed her hands like claws. "What will they do? No one will miss these pirates. It's a good idea, don't you think so?"

Dan wanted to scream. "It's killing people! No, I don't think so."

She glared at him fiercely under her bright hair. "You know, *kuschelbaer*, there are people in this world who could use with some killing."

Dan felt tired and leaned back on the sofa. This night shift life with her took time to adjust to. And then the nights when she got like this. Restless. He felt fried around the edges. Absently he cracked his knuckles with loud pops.

She put her fingers in her ears. "Stop that. Please."

"Sorry."

"You make noises like a pig farmer." She raised her feet onto the chair again and went back to examining her toes. "Gun cases," she muttered. "Ow!" A curling piece of duct tape, one of several plastered over ragged upholstery rips, stuck to the fine hair of her forearm and she tugged it away. A small dribble of sawdust trickled from the exposed gash in the chair, to the floor. "I love this chair and I hate this chair."

Someday he'd have to get her some good furniture, once they figured out where they wanted to live. He wanted that for her. They were always just passing through. They'd stay awhile and then neighbors would get creeped out and soon patrol cars would be snooping around at night and it was time to move on.

Home. Domesticity. That was the ticket. She tried so hard, but it was obvious to him she was losing it. She was becoming insane. She needed grounding, a home, with furniture, with domesticity and a normal life that could heal her. A nice solid house with a sound proofed basement.

"Did you just say 'gun cases'?"

She glanced up from her toes and looked at him, all smiles again, and brushed back her hair. "This movie you brought last week, with the Nicholas Cage, what was it?"

"'Lord of War'."

"Lord of War! This Lord of War, the gun cases, they're like coffins. You see? The pirates, they think they are gun cases, these pirates, they like these gun cases and they open them and—Boom! Big surprise!" She spread her arms, beaming. "Me!"

Where does she keep those special teeth when she isn't using them? he thought. *Even when she smiles you don't see them.*

"And what if they open them in the daylight? Have you ever thought of that?"

It was hard to see her from across the room, in the dim light from the freshly cracked table lamp. Money was getting short. They had a little coming into the bank from the severance package, from his old job on Wall Street, the one he'd lost when he became a little insane too—after she'd picked him out of the herd. But his investments were still sound. They'd be all right for a while. That afternoon he'd landed a shit job running pizzas for Domino's, night shift of course, starting tomorrow evening. She could ride along to keep him company, and he could keep an eye on her. The job didn't pay any benefits, but health insurance wasn't really a problem for her. There wasn't any spare cash to entertain these wild schemes of hers. Funny how, even with a woman like her, the problem was always how much money he made.

He held out his arms to her. "Come here."

She came over to him. As she rose from her beanbag chair, he saw the big ugly hole in the drywall plaster behind her, the one he'd been trying to forget.

She stood in front of him, looking down and gently stroking his hair with her cold fingers. He could feel the tension in her.

"Don't leave me," she said. "That would kill me."

She lay down and stretched out, assertively placing her pretty young girl feet in his lap. Drumming her fingers on her belly nervously, she glanced over at the Jesus clock.

Madness was her greatest fear, she'd said so. He could see why. If a person with her capabilities went over the edge it would be very bad.

Maybe this is how it always ends for someone like that. Over time you carry all this stuff, but you don't know when it will end. You get tired. We're not made to hang around forever. In her way she's very strong. I couldn't do it, I couldn't have just gone on the way she did. If you had any heart, any love, sooner or later that love would just slow you down or poison you until it killed you. She keeps trying to get clean, and that's because she loves me. Everyone else who sees her just sees a pretty fuck. They all want to fuck her. That's how she gets them.

One man in particular—she'd told him—she had put on her little girl lost act for him and drawn him out night after night. She'd played with him and, in his vanity and certainty about the way the world worked, he had allowed her to play with him until he was dead.

4

They never catch on, she'd said. Her smile when she'd said that haunted him whenever he woke early in the afternoon, unable to sleep. He knew these things second hand, as pillow talk in the dawn hours as they lay tangled in sheets.

Home. She just needed a home. She needed him.

In all those years, he was about the only home she'd ever had. This time, in this house, maybe they'd get to stay. A little place in the country like this, away from other people, would be good for them. It was a new start. Now that he had a little job, they were almost plain folks.

"Hey," he whispered. "I saw a magazine ad for this great Vampirella costume. Black patent leather with red trim and these stiletto-heeled riding boots. Very butch. Are you a petite or a medium?"

"*Wie bitte?*" She made a face. "And does it come with a whip?"

"Would you like a whip?"

"What kind of funny magazine do you read? Naked ladies?"

"*Catholic Monthly.*"

"*Verpiss dich.*" She pressed her cold toes against his belly. "Listen to this, funny guy, I want to visit your parents someday. You never want to talk about this. When will you take me to meet your mother?"

"We'll have to work that out."

"Look," he said, as he began rubbing her icy feet. "The pirates are a bad idea. It's not the pirates, it's the idea. You want to go somewhere? Let's go to Italy or someplace nice and get a hotel with a big bed to fuck in and maybe do gravestone rubbings or something, God knows what, but you have to leave people alone."

"I'm not crazy. I'm getting better. I swear. I've got problems. I need you."

5

"The other thing, I know. We'll beat it." He cupped her soft toes, ice cold, in his palms and massaged them, rubbing his hands over her ankles. He bent over and kissed them lovingly. Tickled, she wiggled them against his lips.

"I'm being such a good girl for you."

"Rest in me," he whispered.

"What?" She was daydreaming.

"I was just thinking. I'm your home, *nordchen*. Me. You can rest in me. You haven't had a home for a long time."

"Very long."

"Now you have me. You can heal yourself if you want to."

"Where you are," she said, lifting her foot to touch his nose with her toe, "that's my home."

He kissed her toes again, stretched her feet with his hands and massaged them.

"Did you like my dinner?" she said.

"It was great. You're getting better."

"Who makes better chicken? Me or Popeye Sailor?"

"You, *nordchen*."

She kicked him gently in the thigh and giggled. "You liar. Drink my hair, big fat liar. Pants on fire."

"No, it was really good."

"It could be better if I could taste it. Only it doesn't taste the same to me, like I remember. Drinks taste the same just like anybody, but I can't keep them down."

"How does food taste?"

"Everything tastes like pennies."

"That's how blood tastes to me."

"Isn't that funny?"

"But I liked it fine."

"Because you like me."

"Yes."

6

"And my *muschi*, my pussy-pussy."

"I'd rather eat that than anything."

"That's why you're such a big liar, you want *mien muschi*."

"Do you know Robert Frost?"

"Who?"

"He was this poet. American."

"No."

"He said 'home is that place, that when you go there, they have to take you in'."

"That's you, *kuschelbaer*. No matter what, you always take me in."

A month before, he'd woken up in the early morning, unable to sleep because she had been missing most of the night, and he'd waited up for her until he couldn't stay awake. When he checked her thick curtained little bed to see if she'd come back safe, she was there, looking as bedraggled as a drunk on a binge. There was a single drop of blood on her collar, like a lover's lipstick stain. When she rose later she saw him sitting in a chair in the corner with his face in his hands, weeping. Then she saw the mallet and sharpened wooden mop handle where he'd discarded them, unable to take them up. That night she'd cried her heart out.

"If you can get through this time," he said, "this could be your big chance. I can feed you and you just have to get past, you know, the other stuff. Maybe this is God's grace to you."

"I don't know why God would show grace to me." She looked up at the clock. "You know something? I did laundry early this evening. And then that dryer, it's doing it again, it's making these bubba-bubba-bubba noises and hopping around like a bunny."

"Sounds like that leg on the bottom finally popped off. I'll look at it. We should save up and get a new dryer anyway."

"Hmm."

The noisy Dollar General Jesus clock showed it was after five. The sun would be up in an hour. "It's that time." he heard her whisper. Dan saw her eyes and suddenly made the connection.

Before he could move, she sprang at him. She had him.

Goddamn, she was so fast.

In an instant he was whirled through the air and landed softly but soundly on his back. She stretched on top of him like a pantheress, making a soothing noise that seemed to creep in, making him sleepy. Her steely fingers pinned his arms. The needle sharp fang teeth were out now, gleaming brightly in the light of the abused lamp, pricking and stinging at his throat, as he struggled to look away from the crimson flecked, bottomless wells of her exquisite eyes.

"Now, feed me. *Mein Liebling*."

He wriggled his knees under her, then his feet. Her fangs champed and snapped viciously at his throat. Just as she almost had him, he got his feet against her belly and kicked as hard as he could, flinging her backward through the air. She sailed across the room and crashed into the far wall. The plaster shattered at the impact.

That goddamn cheap-shit drywall! There goes my Sunday.

She slid down, dazed for an instant, then jumped back to her feet like a cat, her fingers clenched into claws of demonic fury. Frantically, he fumbled in his pants pocket. Just as she coiled for the fatal spring, he found it. He thrust it out, almost dropping it. A large mother of pearl crucifix, with a silver Jesus Christ dolefully impaled on its arms. She had said it was gaudy. He liked it anyway.

"Whore of Satan!" he cried "Back, undead vixen! Back to the Hell that cast you out! Back!"

He advanced towards her. She snarled and fell back throwing her arm over her eyes. Then she was moving fast, circling him. "You seek to baffle me with your crosses and your garlic," she sneered murderously. "You with your pale face, to me you are just some fucking sheep in a butcher's!"

Jesus on a bicycle, he thought. *What a cheeseball. She's got that Stoker stuff down pat, too.*

She seized the cheap plastic—replaceable—table lamp and winged it at his hand. He ducked as the lamp knocked the crucifix from his grasp and watched the cross slide out of reach under the sofa. *God forgive me, but I absolutely adore her. If only she could cook.*

She was on him again in an instant. They fell to the floor, clawing and twisting, like Tasmanian devils mating. He grappled for her arms, as her fangs snapped and missed, ripping his shirtsleeve.

His hand slid under the sofa, feeling around frantically. He had the crucifix again. Pulling it out, he shoved it in her face. She jumped off him and he tackled her, sweeping her feet out from under her. They rolled into the table and it went down.

She pushed him off and tore open her T-shirt, exposing her perfect breasts. The urgent pink nipples, erect and rampant, stunned him with lust like a gorgon. Faster than he could see, she swatted his hand. Again, the crucifix flew away from him—no idea where it went this time. He could hardly bear to take his eyes off her tits. He had seen them in various situations, pretty much every night for a glorious year, and they still nailed his feet to the floor every time.

She held him down effortlessly, her breasts dangling in front of his eyes, her knees pinning his shoulders. He wanted to just surrender to her, but first there was one more thing he had to try, just to impress her. He reached into his shirt pocket and took out a simple wooden pencil. Her lips puckered into an O of surprise when she saw it, but it was too late. He pressed the freshly sharpened tip against her heart. "Gotcha!"

He held it there like a knife. She climbed off and backed away from him delicately, her eyes wide with surprise. That was a new move he had thought of while doing a crossword puzzle. Feeling immensely smug, he backed her against the wall. "Strip off your clothes— daughter of Satan!"

Leering, she pulled down her jeans and panties together and dropped them on the floor in a bunch. She was naked now, except for the torn rag of her open T-shirt. She leaned dreamily against the wall, with its broken plaster hole, spreading her legs wide enough for him to see everything, watching him. He kept his eyes fixed on the pencil he held over her heart. If his eyes drifted down to the thick delta of wiry blonde hair between her moist thighs, even for a second, he knew she'd wipe the floor and the dinner dishes both with him.

"Oh don't kill me!" she wailed, wringing her hands. "Don't cast me into Hell—I'll be your slave. My master! I'll do anything you want. Anything! Tell me your desire."

She reminded him of that guy in Star Wars. She'd cried pink tears for Darth Vader when he died.

"On your face!"

She threw herself on the floor, face down, spreading out her body and wiggling her ass. He straddled her and quickly poked the pencil point against her back, over where he figured her heart would be, pressing down slightly so she'd feel it. "Madonna of blood! Devil's slut kitten!"

She shivered under his thighs. Then she trembled. She began to shake, silently. *Okay, 'slut kitten' was pretty bad. Now she has the giggles. She whips those big honeys out and I just can't think straight anymore. She knows it, too.* "I'm still going to punish you as you deserve," he yelled, without conviction.

"Oh—mercy, master," she pleaded, snorting loudly trying to hold it all in. "Beat me, master, I am Satan's blood-soaked whore. Punish me!"

Jesus, now you're just being a smart ass. Go ahead, make fun of me.

He scooted back over her thighs. With the flat of his hand he slapped her butt.

"Ow!" she cried. "Master—punish me harder. Really."

He slapped her ass as hard as he could, swinging from behind.

"Ooh!"

He paddled her again and again, beating her ass with his hand until his wrist began to hurt. Her flesh, technically undead or not, turned a rosy pink under his assault. "I'll punish you!" Whack. "See how I'll punish you for every man you seduced and sent to the grave!" Whap. Whap. "I'll punish your hot little vampire pussy!" Whap

"Ooh! Ow! Punish me, master, I'm so evil!"

"Slut kitten!" *Whatever.*

She buried her face in the carpet and guffawed.

"I'll fuck your fanny, slut kitten of the undead! I'll shove it right up your kazoo!"

"Hey—no! We talked about this," she said firmly. "That is not natural, no. Don't you dare."

"Silence, slave!" Whap.

"Master! Master! Punish me. Pound your wood in my hot little vampire twat—my *muschi*! But not in my ass, I swear. I'll hurt you."

Dan unbuckled his belt and stripped it off. It was wide, black leather studded with little knobs of silver. Installing the silver studs was her idea, and she had insisted to the shoe repair guy they had to be real silver, and very pure, not the fake stuff. If it was fake, she'd know, and if he saw her coming back, he'd better run.

He doubled the belt in his fist and slapped her ass with it hard.

"Yaaah!" She howled sincerely, twisting away in real pain. He reached way, way back and then thinking of that drop of blood on her collar, brought it down on her ass, hard. She screamed passionate obscenities at him in heartfelt German.

He brought the silver studded belt down again and she clawed at the carpet, tearing holes in it with her sharp nails. He rose up and whipped her ass from high up again, the silver studs now raising angry looking red welts on her cheeks and upper thighs.

"Yargh! *Scheisse*—fucking stop!" she bawled, writhing frantically against the floor and, for a moment, he wondered if the neighbors might hear her and call the goddamn cops on them.

"*Nrrgh!*"

"Oh my god, oh my god..." Dan moaned. "I just... baby... I can't wait another second. I need you. I need you so bad."

He yanked down his pants, his hard swollen cock bobbing in the air. "I won't stick it in your ass. But... oh baby. Gimme!"

She suddenly twisted and spun like a cat under him. Before he could take her, she had flipped a window open and vanished. "Come and get me!" she called and was gone.

"Oh...for the luvva..." He picked himself off the floor and tore off the rest of his clothes. He ran for the door, his hard-on waving in front of him. "I'm coming for you honey. God, I love you!"

As he stepped outside, the door slammed behind him. He looked around in amazement and realized what she'd done out here. He'd walked right into her little trap too.

They never catch on.

He looked around. *Now what do I do?*

After they'd become lovers, they'd begun avidly reading vampire novels together from the paperbacks sold at the supermarket. He'd asked her a lot of questions, and it turned out that most of it was a lot of horseshit, but some of the old traditional stuff had a grain of truth in it. She'd teased him with hints and little jokes, but had never really told him all that she could do. Tonight she'd made fog. Unless it was already there. Was it there or did she make it? Could she turn into a bat maybe? Or a wolf? *Jesus, this girl. You just don't know anything about what you're playing with here. For sure you don't ever want this little bitch seriously pissed at you.*

Good fog though.

The house lights were barely visible behind him, as though he were under water. Looking down, he couldn't see his own feet. "Fuck me," he whispered to the dark.

"I hope you're having fun!" he shouted, and hated the tremor in his voice. He moved into the cool white, holding his hands in front of him. "Nixie? Sweet pea?" His erection was fading with honest fear. "I promise I'll fix the dryer."

"*Enfin seuls?*" whispered the breeze.

A wet tongue poked his ear. He spun around, shaking. Sparkling ruby eyes flashed and vanished. Fading laughter in the brilliant moonlit fog.

He took a few more steps and the light of the house faded away. He spun around and couldn't tell in which direction he was facing. He walked his face straight into a tree trunk and cursed. Panic began to quiver his nerves. *When in danger; when in doubt, run in circles, scream and shout? Fuck that. I come from somewhere too; you don't get me without a fight.* He drew a deep breath to focus and began to take up a fighting stance when he heard it coming.

The fast patter of running footsteps in the wet grass. Laughter. A burst. A Tigger-pounce. A collision of lips triumphant, and a hard landing in a bed of pansies in her loving arms.

"*Wie gehts, mein Kuschelbaer*! I've got you—I win, lovie-lovie. *Ach*!" Grabbing him hard by the hair, she buried her face fiercely in his neck and licked him behind the ear, sending jolts of pleasure to his groin. "Do you think I'm going to bite you?" she whispered into his skin "*Jah*? Shall I bite you? Would you like that, no?" She pressed her sharp killing teeth against his skin so he could feel it and ran her tongue over him teasingly. "I'm going to bite you, *leibling*," she said, "and gobble you all up in a wink like the big bad wolfie until you are all gone. Shall I do that? Don't you wonder if you would enjoy that, *jah*?" She put a hand over his cock and he was hard as silk covered steel. "No, no, look what we find down here, oh my goodness; you are not for the biting, no. You are only for loving. *Ich liebe dich!*"

She held him down and this time he didn't fight. Climbing on top of him she arranged herself in a squatting position over his face, working the tip of his nose up in her, filling his senses with her love scent. She wiggled her warm pussy over his face. "You've been so mean to my little ass. You're so cruel to me, I should bite your dick off. Meanie. Kiss it, *Leibling*, please. Make it better."

He pulled her down and worked his tongue up into her pussy, rubbing it against her clit while she sighed and rocked her hips, fucking his face. Taking her clit between his lips, he squeezed it and suckled it while she jumped and growled above him in the fog. Looking up he could see her, pale and gigantic, seeming to reach into the clouds around him and above him. She looked down and tugged at his hair. "What you are looking at? Lick *mein muschi*, that's what you do. Don't you stop or I pull your head off, see if I don't—ah!" She closed her eyes in ecstasy and he drew her in tight, reaching up and holding her breasts in his palms. "*Leck mein Fotze...*don't stop."

As he explored her, feeling her response, pinching and caressing her, she hissed things in German which he couldn't understand. Then he noticed the red welts he'd left all over her cheeks and thighs. They hovered above him like a constellation of red stars, radiating feverish heat. He felt terrible for her and licked them with the flat of his tongue.

"Yah!" She slapped his head. "Stop that." She jerked and he grabbed her hips and pulled her back down tight and sucked her clit until he felt her hips rocking again, sinking into her dream of pleasure. Then he ran the edge of a tooth over a welt and she jumped. "*Arschloch*—I said don't do that!" Her belly was up against his face and he could feel her silently laughing. He lifted her up and, after a moment of licking, ran a tooth over another welt.

"Sonovabitch! I swear— I bite your goddamn head off!"

"Do you have fangs in your pussy too?" he mumbled into her wet labia

"Want to find out?"

15

He slipped his arms under her thighs and tumbled her down onto his face and began to go back and forth between her swollen clit and her swollen welts. She hovered over him on hands and knees. "*Jah*...oh *jah*...that way. Aieee! Damn you! I dare you do that again! Now...*jah*....just do that...oooh... Ow! *Ow*! Fuck! What is wrong with you? Last I warn you this time...*Jah*.....ah...Aiee! *Putz*!"

But her hips were moving faster now. He was on to something. They began a rhythm of licking, moaning, then nipping, cursing, slapping and laughing, and all the while he felt her losing control of her pleasure and pain as her pussy jittered against him frantically. "Nah! *Kom— kom*—pinch my nipples, hurry! Pinch my nipples."

He reached up and took her breasts in his hands and rolled her nipples in his fingertips.

"Now, oh my darling, smiley face! Smiley face!" She shrieked and squeezed her thighs over him stiffly, expiring and sinking down on him with a huge disconsolate sigh. Though he had heard that sigh so many times, he could never fathom the mystery of it. It was the only time she ever breathed. "You're good tonight." she murmured into the smashed pansies.

He rolled her over. She lifted her knees, spreading them, offering herself completely. He kissed each of her breasts and nipped at her neck.

"I'm ready," she said, eyes wide, trembling in anticipation. He seized her hips, and pulled her to him roughly, lifting her thighs up high. She shivered as he touched his knob to her, then slipped in slowly until he felt himself come up against the delicate wall of her virginal skin.

She cringed, which was marvelous to him.

The moment just before he broke through her was the sweetest of rituals. It was the moment he came closest to being what she was, to sharing what they were together. Her fear and desire and his unbearable urge to pierce her with his maleness and conquer her. The little death. It was only then he understood what it was to be her. To need to take down another, to feel them yield to your nature and surrender even to death. He leaned down and pressed his front teeth against her neck. "A little pain," he whispered, "and it will all be over." Her belly tightened and her toes curled.

"Please," she whispered. "Please don't kill me. Please don't kill me, please."

The mystery of her when she talked like this. These odd rituals that had sprung up somehow between them. He had never worked up the courage to ask her what she meant when she begged in these intimate and naked moments between them. Was she mocking words she had heard many times from others? Words that excited her? Or was it because he knew where she slept in the day, inert and helpless? And because the unavenged blood on her hands was in a way on his hands too?

They never catch on.

Each night she required him. Each night she was deflowered. Each night he impaled her. Each night his semen fed her in place of blood. As long as she had his orgasm and seed she didn't need blood, only the eager fountain of his male essence. It was strange to her too. Her pussy palpated around the tip of his cock in anticipation of his gift of pain, life and pleasure. He arched up and pushed through firmly and she gasped and winced as he came through to the root. He held her tight, his heart pounding, his cock pulsing and throbbing at the edge of release as he forced himself to breathe and calm his body. He had to be in control now. He had to be the master of his passions, and not only to be a good lover. If he made a mistake in the next few minutes, she'd kill him without even knowing it.

I read somewhere that the male praying mantis continues to copulate even after the female has bitten off his head. I wonder if that will be true of me?

Deep inside Nixie, his terrible saint, female and carnal, his killer bitch goddess of life and death. Deep inside of her, he held himself still. He rolled her full breasts together and crushed them until the nipples stood out. Her breasts jounced together as he began his cautious, pounding thrusts.

He drew the moment out, and out more, until he could see the pleasure sweeping over her and the line between them began to fade until they were one wounded soul and body.

It was the time. It was this moment, as he felt his ecstasy spreading through him, he always felt the terrible suicidal urge that would probably end in her regaining her senses on some night of love, wailing in grief, with his exsanguinated corpse in her arms. A roll of the dice. A spin of the barrel. Vampire roulette.

Her beautiful blue eyes were turning crimson, half closed in the luxury of pleasure he'd conjured in her. With a vertiginous thrill, like a high trapeze flyer releasing the bar and sailing out into space blindfolded, he allowed himself to fall into her vampiric gaze. Her hypnotic power swept aside his will, mentally stunning him. As the world faded into numbness, as mindless as death, he surrendered his will— his being— to her, and felt her reach out to catch him. She handled his soul, and he allowed her to caress his most intimate spiritual depths with her hidden pain.

His love blazed and released deep inside her and he cried out. Coming back from her spell at the last instant, he braced himself, pushing away from her for what would follow next.

As his seed flowed pulsing into her, she twisted and writhed under him and became some other creature he barely knew. Fighting his body's urge to withdraw and flee, he held his throat as far away from her teeth as he could manage.

She was all over him, beating her arms against him in her savage joy of him. She wanted to get at him with her long teeth, to eat and drink and butcher him with her ravenous love. Sweeter and more nourishing than blood, his semen. It had liberated her from the need for the blood entirely as long as she had his lovemaking to feed her. Like a tiger in a zoo, she didn't need to kill. Their mutual problem was she still *wanted* to. The chase and the kill—it had become who she was. She loved it.

Her vacant eyes rolled up in rapture as she rose on her shoulders, thrusting out her breasts. Her body stiffened and went into a violent seizure. Blindly, she grabbed at his shoulders, raked his back with her nails. The hot blood ran down his spine and he rolled frantically to the side to keep it away from her lips, without letting her get on top of him. Each night, in these crucial moments, she reminded him of how terribly he now wanted to live.

The adrenaline rush was beyond anything he had ever felt on the Wall Street trading floor back in the day. They were slaves to each other's flesh, addicted to the other's unique gifts, a mortal bargain they had entered into freely. Her spine arched, bones creaked in the extremity of her pleasure and her mouth gaped unnaturally wide, showing her killing fangs. The sight of them provoked his loins to a second orgasm in some terrified, ancient response.

As she received his seed again, she relaxed and sagged. He hugged her tight, pinning her arms to her sides, and buried his face in her bosom as she bore him back down to the ruined flowerbed.

Mutually sated, against all odds still alive, they were—in their way—the happiest couple in the world.

* * * *

Jessebel

© Sacchi Green

"See there, Cap'n, ain't she somethin'? Jezebel, they calls 'er, but most likely she's just plain Mabel or Hildy underneath it all."

I looked through the drifting cigar smoke and shifting bodies. Maybe three or four of those figures were recognizably female—for damned sure not counting my own well-concealed form—but there was no doubt as to which one had sparked the old stable hand's enthusiasm. I couldn't see much; her back was to the door, and a rancher's burly arms enveloped her in a most unchaste fashion as they danced, but even so there seemed to be a glow about her that drew the eye. Chestnut curls tumbled across slender shoulders, and emerald silk clung to rounded, swaying hips that promised the uttermost in carnal delights without sacrificing the least degree of elegance.

"Sure is, Bill," I agreed, "but what's a fine piece like that doing in a place like this?"

"Plenty of business, that's what." Bill elbowed me in the ribs. I only just managed to pivot enough to keep my bound-up tender bits from taking the full impact. When I turned back the girl swung around so that for a moment, before her partner's bulk blocked the view, I saw her face, beautiful in spite of all its paint, not because of it.

The room swirled around me. The floor tilted. I clutched at the back of a chair, muttered an apology to the card player occupying it, and lurched back out through the swinging doors.

The last time I'd kissed that face it had been ashen, dirt-smeared, streaked with blood and my tears. The last time I'd held that dear body in my arms, life and warmth had seeped away.

The last time I'd seen her, she'd been dead.

Great gulps of cool autumn air revived me a bit. The dizziness subsided, and common sense got a foothold. I'd been mistaken, addled by smoke and old grief and going far too long without the pleasures of the flesh. Maybe the name, as well, far too close to the one I remembered. That painted, seductive, brazen whore looked nothing like Jessebel. Not my Jess. My Jess, who was gone forever. I knew that.

I was only too well acquainted with death. I knew it when I saw it, and all the savage ways war could rip the soul out of the body. War, and its aftermath. Jess and I had been together since Vicksburg, when I'd found her huddling in a farmer's root cellar, gray uniform in such tatters that it scarcely hid her private parts. She'd been running away not just from capture but from something else she could never bring herself to speak of. I'd scrounged her a blue uniform small enough to fit, and watched over her for the last two years of the War, only to lose her to a looter's bullet before we could start west to make a real life for ourselves.

"Cap'n?" Old Bill poked his head out. "You okay?"

"I'll be right fine in a minute or two. Town crowds take some getting used to when a fellow's been up in the mountains so long."

"I s'pose that's so," Bill said doubtfully.

I fished out a coin from my pocket and sent it spinning. He forgot anything else in the catching of it. "You go on and order that drink," I said, "and if you've downed it before I get to the bar, I'll just be obliged to buy you another one to go with mine."

Bill knew well enough that I'd be good for three or four drinks anyway, but he hared right back inside to get an early start. The old fellow was my habitual bridge to human society on my twice-yearly expeditions out of the mountains. In the spring I'd be bringing in the fruits of my trap lines to the fur traders, and in the autumn I'd stock up on whatever winter needs my gun wouldn't supply.

Either way, my horse and mule would get put up at the livery stable where Bill worked, and Bill would fill me in on whatever versions of world and local news were being bandied about. It gave me a chance to get accustomed to another human voice without having to exercise my own too much all at once. He'd always taken me at face value, too, never questioning the shabby Union Captain's uniform I'd ridden in with three years ago, and neither had anybody else.

The Union part was right enough, and I'd worn a uniform throughout the war, as had a fair number of other females I'd encountered or heard tell of, besides Jess. But the clothes I'd worn at the last had come from an officer who would never need them again. Leather and fur and two new flannel shirts a year suited me better now.

Bill's big news this time had been the new girl at the Hard Ride Saloon. The girl who... I got a firm grip on my wandering mind. She wasn't Jess. And she wasn't for me. The tawdry regulars at the Hard Ride were good enough old girls, but I'd never yet trusted one of them with my personal...eccentricities, and I wasn't about to start now with a flashy stranger who'd look more at home in New Orleans or San Francisco.

As I pushed through the saloon door I did, however, wish fleetingly that I'd bought my semiannual new shirt already, and gone to the trouble of visiting the local bathhouse out behind the barber shop.

At the bar I ordered a whiskey, gestured for Bill's glass to be refilled, and only then turned, leaned back, and viewed the room as a whole. Or tried to, but somehow the scarlet woman in emerald green drew the eye, as if all the light shone particularly on her, or even from her. It wasn't just me, either. Seemed like every man in the house was watching and panting after her, and those card players whose chairs faced the wrong way were continually hitching themselves around to steal a look. If I could've looked away myself I'd have considered playing some poker just to take advantage of the general befuddlement and inattention to serious business.

Bill wiped his sleeve across his mouth, ready to take a short pause from knocking back his liquor. "See? Ain't she a corker, just like I said? I s'pose she'll move on soon's she's emptied the pockets 'round here, and wore out a few more big spenders."

"A few more?" The man with her was perspiring, but hardly looked worn out. More like pumped up fit to burst, which was entirely understandable. Her dress was so fancy and fine a fellow might be afraid to touch it, but the way her body moved roused a powerful urge to rip her clothing right off. I was in as bad a case as any, but in my own way, with damp heat throbbing between my thighs and a maddening pressure building in my bound breasts.

"Yes indeed, she's had more'n one stumblin' around like a winded horse after a night with her. Old Dunlap at the bank was so bad his heart near stopped, and he ain't even been able to speak a word since. But he'd been sickly for quite a while, and should have known better, the old sot."

Maybe she felt our attention on her, maybe it was just by chance, but suddenly, as the piano player paused to mop his brow and the dance music stopped, her eyes looked right straight into mine. Great gray eyes with long lashes needing no artifice to darken them.

Eyes that knew me.

The light in them flickered. Her practiced smile froze. This time I was stunned instead of dizzy, and before I could move she tugged her partner toward the staircase. In his eagerness he came near to carrying her up to the gallery above, while she clung to him and hid her face in his shoulder.

Rage, lust, and an eerie horror filled me, each so strong it didn't seem possible one heart and mind could hold any of them. I surged forward, staring upward. My breath caught when she looked down at me for a mere instant, and in that heartbeat I saw my Jess as I'd so often seen her—pale, hungry, brave in the face of danger, hair cropped like a boy's, lovely gray eyes aglow with love—and then there was only a glimpse of chestnut curls and emerald silk. And then she was gone.

"Cap'n!" Bill was clinging to my belt. I was halfway up the stairs, in such a daze I didn't recall getting there. Other, stronger hands tugged at me, the saloon owner's hired bullyboys. I'd have taken them on one at a time, being as tall as the average man and about as hefty, but I had just enough sense left not to tackle a crowd, or be tackled by one.

"Hold your horses, chum," one of them said amiably enough. "Go sleep it off. Maybe you'll get lucky tomorrow, if you've got the cash. Her Highness don't take but one beau a night."

I subsided, and let myself be pushed out the door. Bill still hung close by, so I waved him off and said I needed time to clear my head, and would move along to my bed in the boarding house soon.

"I was sure enough right, wasn't I just!" he said in parting. "That fancy filly is really somethin'! Somethin' else!"

Oh God, yes, I thought. *Something else, But what?*

I had to know. And whatever the explanation, or whatever...whatever she'd become, I had to see Jess again.

In the narrow alley behind the saloon I moved along stealthily, listening, trying to make out which upper room held Jess and her customer. A forced giggle through the first window was clearly from one of the other girls. On the far end, though, sounds so urgent and guttural they made my innards clench struck me like a brutal blow. They were hard at it. Jess's soft, high moans that I remembered so well could be heard in between the man's deep grunts of extremity. When those finally tapered off I could still hear Jess, her cries oddly muted now, as if her mouth were pressed to him.

I was in such a state of heat that I could've rubbed myself off right there, but my need to get to Jess was even greater. The alley was so narrow here that the low shed in back was scarcely more than an arm's reach from the window, so I hoisted myself onto its roof and looked across.

The light of an oil lamp showed Jess's bowed head as she knelt beside the bed, and just a glimpse of the now-quiet man. By the tremor of her naked back and shoulders she seemed to be sobbing, whether in grief or pleasure, but at that moment I didn't care which. I just hungered to feel her touch on *me*, her mouth crushing down hard where my pounding need was so intense it burned, her fingers squeezing into flesh demanding to be unbound, her rounded buttocks filling my hands.

Then she raised her head, and I saw her wipe a trickle of blood from the corner of her mouth. The brute had hit her! She saw me at just the same time, sprang up, and threw open the window. "Oh God, Lou... help me!"

I was through and into the room so fast I had no time to think about it. The man on the bed didn't stir. What help did she need, whoever...whatever...she was now?

"Lou!" Jess's eyes had a strange, glazed look, and she scrabbled at the lacings of the tight corset she still wore. "Lou, please!"

I got right at the garment, tearing and peeling, looking for injuries, but her body beneath was unmarked by anything beyond the normal lines and creases such fashionable instruments of torture impart. Before I could halfway finish Jess kept interfering, grasping at my hands, trying to press them to her breasts, her belly, and the hot sweet cleft below.

"Touch me, damn it! Fuck me!" Her voice was rough with urgency. "He was so...such hot blood...so full..."

I tried to stop her talk with a kiss, but her head jerked sideways, so I dropped my head to her breasts and sucked fiercely at one extended nipple and then the other. That did the trick, and I managed to finish stripping her, hard though it was with her demanding thrusts and whimpers and the swelling of her flesh against my tongue.

When I was finally free to get at all of her skin, she writhed and panted and seemed to demand everything at once, pulling my hands here and there and here again, grabbing at her own tender bits when I clutched at her elsewhere, until I tore off my shirt, yanked up the bindings of my breasts, and held her so tightly against me she could scarcely move.

"Hold still so's I can get at you!" I was in a frenzy of lust myself by then, with her wriggles against my own nipples coming near to undoing me, but I pushed her back against the wall, got my fingers between us and right into the wet heat of her center, and gave her what she needed with the sure, hard strokes that had always driven her to glory. She got there right away, riding the peak hard and long, gasping and crying out until she had no breath left, but still clenching me inside her fit to bruise. I began to fear she'd faint from it.

She slumped finally enough for me to reclaim my hand. Then she rested her head against my breast, which of course kept my flesh perked right up. I figured she was too wrung out to give me a turn yet, and wasn't sure how I could bear it. But after a moment she twisted out of my grip, dragged me toward the bed with a strength she'd never shown before, and heaved at the sheets until the man lying there tumbled to the floor on the other side. He still didn't stir. I didn't look close for fear of what I wasn't prepared to see, not while Jess was pulling at my belt and pushing me onto the mattress.

I got my turn, right enough, but in snatches between Jess's fits of renewed desire. She rubbed her body all over mine, took a goodly expanse of breast into her mouth, tweaked my imploring clit between her fingers, and then got distracted by the need to grind herself against my hip or belly or rump until she exploded again. And again. And again. I was streaked all over with her juices. She was insatiable, beyond thought or pleading. I was in such a fury of lust myself that it didn't take much to set me off, and when she rode my thigh with her knee pressed tight into my crotch, or when I could hold her right over me so that her writhings hit in just the necessary spot, I went off like firecrackers too, more times than I'd ever done before.

Finally Jess slowed enough that I could hold her face steady down where I needed it most. Once her tongue got a taste of my flow she set to working me in steady strokes that got me riding a long, rolling wave of pleasure that ended only when my breath and voice gave out.

28

She hitched herself up beside me at last and clung tight, her face hidden between my neck and shoulder. "Lou," she murmured, "I don't want to hurt you. Don't ever let me hurt you."

I stroked her long tangled curls, new to me even though the texture and scent of her hair had been imprinted in my heart long ago. "I've never minded any hurt from you before."

"Things are different now. So different..." Her tears were hot against my throat.

"I know." Just as I knew that Jess had been dead, and was now alive. And that the man on the floor was dead, permanently. Back in Connecticut, when they talked of vampires, nothing like Jess came to mind, but there must be some ancient truth behind such stories. "You'd better tell me about it later. You need to get away from here before they find him on the floor. I'll be right along, but it's best they don't connect us. Too many here have a general notion of where I hole up in the winter."

So I lowered Jess from the window, and she disappeared into the shadows, wrapped in a dingy blanket. Twelve hours later I was on my way, mule and horse loaded with sacks of cornmeal and bacon and ammunition and all such winter supplies. Three miles down the trail I paused to water my critters where a tangle of brush rimmed a small creek, and when we resumed our travel Jess was perched up in front of me. My old Jess, in boy's clothes stolen from some laundry yard and chestnut hair chopped short and ragged—yet not the old Jess.

"Back in town they're using that word," I told her, not quite wanting to say it myself. "The doctor says the fellow's blood was drained so low he couldn't live."

"Vampire, that's the word. Might as well call it that; the old woman that raised me did, said I had the taint,

29

though there was no way to tell how it might turn out. That's all I know. Never knew any family. Never felt any difference, nor special powers, nor... nor needs, not until I was dead—and then I wasn't dead."

I held my arm tighter around her middle. "How does it work? Does it pass on to...to whoever?" For a moment I wondered whether Jess's blood would taste different now than when I'd kissed the streaks on her face as she'd died.

"Not that I've noticed yet. Not from just once, anyway. That fellow last night, well, I went too far. I didn't mean to. But I was distracted on account of seeing you, and wild to get filled up before you got to me so I wouldn't need to, well, hurt you."

I pondered that for a while. "How often do you...well, how often do you need it?"

"Depends on a lot of things. I can get by with animals, but it's not the same. Even with folks it's not always the same. After that old banker, I felt near as sick as he did, but that fellow last night, so pumped up with lechery— well, that was really something."

"Sure was." I savored the recollection. "Anything else I should know?"

"Plenty I should know myself but don't. I'm working my way west, hoping maybe in San Francisco there's some like me I can learn from."

"Time enough for that when winter's past. The mountain passes are already getting snow. We'll manage fine in my cabin."

Jess didn't object, just settled more comfortably against me. We'd manage, with the critters I shot for food. If it came to it, I knew where a she-bear denned for her winter's sleep, and if her blood made Jess sleepy too in the dead of winter, that might be just as well. Any time my own blood rose, I was pretty sure I could get Jess to indulge enough to get her going. The thought of her teeth sinking into my neck, or my breast, or my belly, got me shifting in the saddle already.

She wouldn't go on to San Francisco alone, either. If it suited her to be Jessebel there, in fine silks and corsets, well, I could handle that, and even put on fine gent's togs to match. Didn't matter who, or what, she was to anybody else. Our bond held. She'd always be my Jess.

Although I did wonder just how long "always" might turn out to be.

* * * *

My Soul to Take
© Kimber Vale

The pine box was simple, smaller than average. Although not as diminutive as the children's coffins he had buried over the past five years, it was significantly shorter than the box that would one day hold him for his final repose.

When the pallid lad in the outdated and ill-fitting suit rang the bell at half-past midnight, Father Michael McCredie was too groggy to properly question the young man.

"Me mistress bid me return the carriage right quick but I'll lend ye a hand movin' 'er in."

"What is this? No arrangements have been made for a body tonight." The priest scowled, his arms crossed against his chest.

The embalmers took the emergency calls any time, night or day. Father Michael, however, usually received the deceased during business hours in order to perform burials. There was no need for such a disturbance in the wee hours of the night. No odor emanated from the casket. This person did not need to rush to the grave.

"Lady Maeve Belus." The boy pushed the door wider and picked up the casket with a grunt. His strength was surprising for one so thin. In fact, "undernourished" was the word Father Michael associated with the scrawny, sunken-eyed youth. In sympathy, the priest grabbed the rope handle on one end and shuffled backwards into the church.

There were benefits to lodging in the tiny apartment behind the church. The price was certainly right. But on this night, the half-pound he saved each month hardly seemed worth the interruption to his sleep. He would get the coffin inside and deal with it in the morning. A stern word would need to be sent to the embalmer.

But who had sent her?

Father Michael turned to question the lad but he had vanished into the inky darkness. The weary priest barred the heavy front door with a sigh.

Blast it! Better not make a habit of this.

What name had the boy given? Maeve Belus, wasn't it? The appellation sounded familiar, but the priest did not recall it being on the schedule for the following day. Perhaps this poor soul was to be interred two days hence? There was no reason for the preparers to send her to him in the black of night, in any case.

Curiosity ate at him as he shuffled toward his room. The name was a bell tolling ceaselessly in his head. He would not sleep until his questions were answered.

The book listing all special services was a musty old tome. Names of infants to be baptized were scrawled alongside those of the dead awaiting their eternal resting place. Occasionally, when the fates were cruelest, there were tiny children on the pages awaiting the prayers for the dead. Weddings and confirmations punctuated the pages, but those were less frequent than the comings and goings of bodies.

The babes squirmed and kicked, squalling to the heavens when Father Michael sprinkled the cleansing water on their heads. They grew red-faced with anger as they were anointed with the sacred oils. He could not help but smile when he christened the complainers. They did not know how fortunate they were.

Ashes to ashes, dust to dust. Since leaving the seminary and joining Immaculate Conception Church, Father Michael felt most moved by the last rights. His youth never tasted as sweet as when he buried the dead.

But who was this lady in such a hurry to block out the last rays of sun? His list did not contain the hauntingly familiar name given by the delivery boy. Perchance he had buried a relative of hers in the past?

He flipped through the book backwards, knowing the niggling doubt he felt would not give him peace tonight. Name after name, but none matched.

Belus was an unusual surname, and one he did not find in his registry. Maeve, however; was well-used in Ireland. A warrior queen by the same name was prominent in an epic twelfth century manuscript. Mab or Maeve. Father Michael had read the old prose in school. The tale had made an impression on him, and more so when he learned his own Mab had died.

Perhaps the name was no more familiar than that, the derivative of *her* name, the girl he had loved and lost before entering the seminary. He *had* loved her, but not enough to save her. Not enough to deny his calling to the priesthood.

They had shared a night of youthful passion. Mab had thought the act could sway him, but Michael viewed it as a parting gift before his life of servitude began. It was something to remember in the celibate years ahead. He took what she offered because it was more than he could do to resist. Letting her go had broken his heart, but his faith sustained him in his grief.

He did not discover Mab had committed suicide until he returned to County Cavan after his years of study.

The morbid tale was the sensation of the county. A jilted young woman sliced her wrists to shreds and bled to death in the woods. Five years after the event, folks still spoke of it. Father Michael did not believe that the gossips attached his name to the girl, but it did not matter. He would always feel responsible for her death.

34

His entrance into the church would forever be tarnished by his guilt.

Father Michael closed the worn book with conviction. The familiarity of the name was only a result of the blame he felt. The realization left him exhausted, and heartsick he trudged off to his bed.

* * * *

In the pitch black sanctuary, iron nails popped from the knotted planks and dropped to the floor like heavy tears. The casket slid open with a whisper and the raven-haired woman sat up. She gazed around the room, her eyes easily distinguishing objects despite the lack of light. The smell of piety assaulted her senses, singeing her nose. The life-sized cross above the pulpit caused a hiss to sizzle from her ruby lips. But she had been invited in, and none of the trappings of religion could hurt her tonight.

She jumped from the coffin, her landing graceful and cat-like, and then Mab slipped silently through the church.

Michael tossed to and fro on the bed, his sleep tortured. She watched him for many minutes, savoring the long-awaited sight of him—reveling in his imminent capture.

Her arms had not been enough to hold him when she was human. Her love was no match for the love of his God. But she had waited patiently, allowing his guilt and celibacy to wear on him. This night was destined. The moment tasted finer than blood. Her body would be the only altar he would worship at from this point on. The excitement humming through her was akin to the pinnacle before an orgasm. She knew bliss was moments away, but planned to draw it out. She would enjoy every succulent morsel of Father Michael's corruption.

35

The evening gown she wore dipped low, its contours shaped by the corset that pushed her breasts into porcelain mounds and nearly spilled them from the bodice. The red satin fell in gathered pleats about her waist, but she wore no bustle beneath. The contraption did not fit well in coffins. The dead need not follow the mandates of fashion. Indeed, she had declined to wear shoes in the wooden box.

The young thrall who had delivered her had not questioned her impropriety. His bones ached to be consumed by her and his infatuation made him a perfectly obedient, if tedious companion.

She watched Michael's imperfect slumber from the foot of his bed.

She did not want to scare him. He would discover her true nature soon enough. First, she wanted him to taste the temptation of a flesh and blood woman and be unwilling to stop himself. Afterward, he would sample the seduction of eternal life with his undead bride. She wanted him on his knees, pleading for mercy, yet unable to say no. She would never take second place to his God again.

Skirt hiked to her hips, she mounted him slowly, softly, feeling his warm weight shift beneath her and mold to her body while he slept. Without conscious thought he chose her, chose to accept the basic animal need that flowed through his veins and taunted every muscle in his body. She leaned forward, watching the vessel on his neck thrum with life. It called to her, the pull magnetic and seductive. She licked her lips, feeling razor-sharp teeth scrape against her tongue.

Control. She had come to exert it over him, but she must keep a firm grip on her own desires, otherwise she would be the one eternally grieving her dead lover. And she did not want him dead. No, he would become as she was so he could remember the choice he had made for all eternity.

"Michael." Her lips brushed his carotid artery as she whispered his name. The close proximity to warm blood sent a shiver through her. A nearly undeniable need gnawed at her being.

Reluctantly, Mab moved away from the strong pulse. She found his earlobe with her tongue and flirted the wet tip over the soft, peach-fuzz skin. He groaned her name in his sleep and her deadly smile answered his call.

His face was sculpted and strong with a hint of beard around his jaw. The short hairs peppered down the crease that ran from his lower lip to his chin. It was new since she last kissed him, when he was more boy than man, a shade of red-brown that did not quite match the dark waves on his head.

Thankfully she liked it, as it would never change again after this night. Mab knew his eyes were the same mesmerizing mahogany behind his closed lids.

"Mab," he mumbled, and she pressed her lips against his, thrilling in their heat and the scratchy stubble surrounding them. She kissed him long and deep, running a tongue over his lips until they parted. His warm, wet tongue met hers with a too-brief abandon. And then the sudden tension in his body alerted her to his full awakening. She pulled away to gaze into his dark eyes.

"Is it truly you? How can this be?" He leaned over to light a lantern beside his bed. She allowed him the movement. He could not possibly escape her. His human strength and speed were no match for her own, despite her petite size and his strapping six-foot frame.

Michael turned back to her, taking in her face, his gaze lingering on the exposed thighs that straddled him. He grabbed her wrists in search of scars, and ran his fingers wonderingly over smooth flesh.

"It is I. Never any other." She grasped his hand and cupped it against her breast. His manhood stirred beneath her and she sighed with satisfaction.

"I have missed you." She spoke softly, careful not to expose her sharp canines. Slowly she rubbed his palm against her stiff nipple as her other hand reached out to smooth a wavy lock from his brow. Her cool fingertip trailed down his temple to tease his lower lip.

"And I you, Mab. But I do not understand..."

"Shhhhh." She pressed her lips against his once more, ravenously kissing away his misgivings. Again his cock surged beneath her in response. She snaked a hand between his legs and stroked him through the bedcovers while she kissed a hot path down his neck.

"Mab, I made my vows. This bed shall not be defiled. I cannot lie with you again." He sucked in his breath as she pulled the tie open on the front of his night shirt and her mouth found his nipple.

"I was wrong to take your innocence without a promise of matrimony," he added in a choked whisper.

She gave a quick nip at his tender flesh and felt her canines superficially pierce his skin.

Mab sat up, perilously close to losing control from the faint salty taste that swirled in her mouth and made love to her tongue.

With a growl, she ripped wide the front of his linen shirt and fully exposed his strong chest. Grasping her gown above each breast, she rent the fabric down the center. The ruined satin she shrugged off and tossed to the floor in a dejected heap.

Fear crept into his gaze. But naked lust also burned in his eyes as they devoured her black lace corset. Aside from the red ribbon tied fashionably around her neck she wore nothing else.

"When I take *your* innocence, Michael, I will not be as heartless as you were. I vow to keep you as my spouse for the rest of time." She smiled down at him, no longer hiding her true nature.

"What have you become?" His voice was a hoarse whisper.

"Your darkest desire, my love. Life everlasting. I was nearly gone. My heart struggled to beat as my blood leaked into the ground. And then Baal came up from the red earth and saved me. He showed me that eternal life would be denied me by your God. He gifted me with his own blood so that I can live forever and grant the same gift to whomever I choose."

"The Prince of Darkness? He speaks lies with a forked tongue!"

"And yet here I am." She trailed a wet tongue from his naval to his nipple to lick the drying drop of blood that welled at the small puncture mark. Her body trembled with desire as she moved to his other nipple to swirl around the tight peak before she slowly kissed her way back down his abdomen.

"If ever you loved me, Mab, leave me now." His breathing was shallow. She slid back and yanked the coverlet down to expose his hard cock.

"Please." With voice and eyes he pleaded, but whether he prayed she cease or continue, she could not say. When her hand wrapped around his hard length he shuddered. A drop of moisture waited on his tip and she lowered her mouth to it. Teasingly slow, she licked the salty pearl and watched his stare follow her tongue.

The priest's hips arched toward her mouth as she pulled away. His body silently begged for more.

Mab pulled his thick ridge into her mouth. Intensely she sucked the head of his organ, feeling the blood flooding hot and hard beneath his skin. His thick cock swelled her cheeks, testing her willpower. Her nails dug into his hips as she strove to dominate the fierce need to bite—the hunger that demanded she suck every last drop from him. *Not yet.* She took him deep in her throat, cupping his full balls while he surged in and out between her lips, his breathing erratic and tormented. His hands fumbled with the laces on the front of her corset before he gave up and slid his fingers inside to pinch her nipples.

She needed more.

Mab ripped the ties of the corset as if they were paper. A tremendous sense of freedom seized her as her unbound wings rose in a black cloud above her head. Their leather unfurled to the width of outstretched arms. Like a stalking predator she crawled up his naked body, rubbing her hard nipples along the length of him until they were face to face.

"I am what you made me." She rubbed her lower lip against his. Her nails combed through his hair and scraped down the back of his neck.

"I want your tongue inside me. I want to wrap my legs around your head and feel your warm breath burning the inside of my thighs." Her voice was a demanding whisper against his ear.

She sucked on his earlobe as if it were his cock, and then teased inside with her tongue. Michael's hands kneaded her hips to grind her wet pussy against his stomach. She could feel him hard and ready, nudging her backside. But first she required complete submission. He pulled her up toward his mouth, as willing as any thrall.

His tongue was hotter than she imagined, slick and sure, as it entered her hole in a series of quick thrusts before sliding up and down the length of her slit. She panted despite having no need for oxygen. When she grasped his modest bedposts, her fingertips etched divots in the wood. Dull teeth nipped at her clit and she cried out in surprise before he drew her throbbing nub inside. He sucked her with animal force, his tongue flicking against her sensitive peak, so fast it seemed inhuman. Tears, surprising and rare, welled in her eyes.

Her breath tumbled out in rapid waves. A habit from her human life, it reminded her of their last encounter together. The sweat and saliva, the gasping for air as they launched each other into paradise, were forever imprinted upon her memory. The heart in her chest no longer beat, but still he made her feel exquisitely alive.

Head back, she howled with her orgasm. Michael gripped her small waist and led her down toward his thick cock while her muscles clenched with release. He pushed inside her tight, wet folds, groaning against her ear. His husky exclamations of pleasure were portentous music in the still church.

Rock hard yet so smooth, his cock was armor clad in a silken sheath. He rolled his hips against her, teasing her throbbing clit as he slid in and out. Mab had planned to control him, but now he led the dance. Pulling her up and down on top of his stiff rod he worked himself to climax. She felt him ready to explode and leaned in for the culmination of their lovemaking.

His cock pumped rhythmically, pouring out his warm seed deep inside her. Mab tilted his face, exposing his neck while he came. Her fangs pierced him. He pitched beneath her in a marriage of futile resistance and lingering rapture. She drank deeply of his lifeblood, until his heartbeat was shadow-fragile, his body still as a corpse.

His expression was peaceful, painted with bliss. Michael would die content if she abandoned him now, as he had her. But Mab sliced a gash at her wrist with knife-edged teeth and held the wound to his pale, parted lips. His body quivered beneath her as the remaining vestiges

41

of mortality reluctantly flew off. When her priest hungrily began to suckle at the ragged flesh, Mab pulled away and folded him inside her powerful embrace.

Leather wings beat the air, pulling them up into the purple-black sky. The vampires rose into the night to greet their dark eternity. They would rest in one another's arms as the sun shifted across the horizon, but the next creeping dusk would mark the beginning of Father Michael's endless new calling.

* * * *

Willing
© Xan West

I slam him against the wall. Bring out my knife. Whisper words across his skin, the steel teasing, tempting. Kick his legs apart. The blade ripping through his shirt, tormenting, aching to slice him open. Up close breathing on his neck, teeth almost breaking skin. Step back slapping, leaving a handprint on his cheek. My knife at his throat. My hand covering his mouth. My eyes on his. Feeding on his helplessness. Feeding on his fear. A slow smile creeping across my face as I begin. My fist driving into his pecs. My gloved hand slapping his face. His nipple twisted between my fingers, hot under my teeth. Turned over, face against the exposed brick of the wall. My fist on his back, methodical. My boot ramming into his ass. My open hand menacing him with slaps. My cock throbbing hard as I press into him and bite down on his shoulder, holding back, yet feeding on his pain. I ride with him as I pull out my tools, laying into his back... until I am ready to thrust the pain home with my quirt. Driving welts into his back, we will soar together, gliding on his pain, his helplessness, my power, our pleasure. And when we are done flying, he will be on the floor at my feet, tongue wrapped around my boot.

It will do. The beast inside me calls for flesh, for pain. He is demanding and relentless and I barely keep him in check. It's better if they choose it. Want it. It adds a certain something that is indescribable and yet has become necessary to the meal. So I keep him sated with sadism, feeding on fear and pain and sex and helplessness. Once, I was waiting for the willing. That illusive willing boy I might call my own. I no longer hope for him. He does not exist.

Now, I find boys at The Lure. Boys like this one, who want to open themselves to my tools. But sometimes that is not enough to take the edge off. Sometimes it just stokes the hunger. When the urge for blood becomes incontrollable I return to Gomorrah, looking for those hungry eyes, the pulse in a boy's throat that shows he wants it. It's hard to keep a straight face here, amidst the pretenders, the elitist pseudo vampires, the Stand and Model version of SM, the Sanguinarium, the followers of the Black Veil. So it's a last resort, this feast of image and fantasy. When the beast must feed and pain is not enough.

I stride to a shadowed corner and watch for food. The rhythm of the music brings a booming to my brain as my eyes slide along the flesh exposed, watching for that look, that swiftly beating pulse in his throat.

Whispers begin as I am glimpsed by the regulars, and I know all it will take is a crook of my head and a smoldering gaze. It's too easy here. I am not seen. I am simply a fantasy come true, made all the more fantastic by my refusal to be showy in dress or demeanor. A growl of disgust rolls through me. I choose my meat, a tall broad-shouldered goth boy with long black hair and a carefully trimmed beard. I draw him to me, and lead him out to the alley. He thinks this is a quick fuck, and drops to his knees. My hand grips him by that delicious hair and yanks him up, tossing him against the wall. I want to savor this meal. He needs to last.

I pull out my blade and show it to him. His eyes widen and he whispers, "My safeword is chocolate." I am surprised. Most who frequent the fetish scene know nothing about real BDSM. That these are the first words out of his mouth shows that there may be more to this boy than I thought. I stand still, watching him. He is older than I had first surmised, at least twenty four. The little leather he wears is well kept, his belt clearly conditioned and his boots cared for by a loving hand. He is motionless, knees slightly bent, shoulders back, offering me his chest. His pulse is not rapid, but his eyes eat up the knife and his lips are slightly parted, as if all he wanted was to take my blade down his throat.

His brown eyes stay fixed on the knife as I move toward him. I tease his lip with the tip of it and then speak softly.

"How black do you flag?"

His eyes stay on the blade. He swallows.

"Very black, on the right, Sir."

"Is there anything I need to know?"

"I am healthy and strong. My limits are animals, children, suspension and humiliation, Sir."

"And blood, hmmm?" I am teasing. I know the answer. It is why I found him here, and not at the Lure.

"Oh please, Sir. I would gladly offer my blood."

"Why?"

He takes a deep breath, closes his eyes a moment, and then opens them. The pulse in his throat starts racing, but his voice is calm, and matter-of-fact. I tease my blade against his neck.

"I have been watching you a long time, Sir. I have seen how you play. I see the beast inside you. I know what is missing. Those boys at The Lure don't know how to give you what you really need. They don't see that they are barely feeding your craving, and not touching your hunger. The boys here don't see you. They just see their own fantasy. They are simply food. I am strong, Sir. Strong enough for you. I can be yours. My blood, my flesh, my sex, my service. Yours to take however you choose, for as long as you want. To slake your hunger. I would be honored, Sir."

I take a deep breath, stunned, studying him. This boy who would offer what I never really thought was possible. He has surprised me again. That alone shows this boy is more than a meal. He just might be able to be all that he has offered.

I almost leave him there. I am ready to walk away. Fear creeps along my spine. With the centuries I have lived and the things I have seen, this boy is what scares me. There is nothing more terrifying than hope. I rake my eyes over him. He is standing quietly. He looks like he could stand in that position for hours. He has said his piece; he is content to wait for my response. Oh, he is more than food, this one. What a gift to offer a vampire. Can I refuse this offering when it's laid out before me? I step back, looking him over, and decide.

I breathe in possibility, watching the pulse in his throat. My senses heighten further as I focus my hunger on him, noticing the minute changes in breath, scenting him. I want to see him tremble. I want to smell his fear. I want to devour his pain, without holding back. Forget this public arena. If there is even a possibility that I might truly let go and move with the beast inside my skin, his growl on my lips and his claws grasping prey, I know exactly where I need to take this boy.

I put the knife away, pull the black handkerchief from his back pocket and wrap it around his head, covering his eyes. He cannot see the way to where we are going. He has not earned that much trust. I grip him by the back of the neck and lead him to my bike. When I start the engine, its growl answers me, echoing off the walls of the alley. I take the long way, through twists and turns of the back streets, enjoying the wind on my face and the purr of the bike.

We are here. I ease him off the bike and lead him by the neck down the stairs into the lower level of the brownstone. It is a large soundproof room. There are no windows. It is one big tomb. Every detail is designed for my pleasure, down to the exposed brick wall installed for the simple gratification of slamming meat against it. This room is where I sleep, and where I take my prey when I want privacy.

Private play means I let my hair down, and roam free, claws unsheathed. I leave him in the doorway, and ready myself, breathing deep, and freeing my hair. I strip off my shirt so I can feel the hair brush my lower back. It is my vanity, and I have worn it long for centuries, no matter the current fashion.

I keep him blindfolded, and throw him against the wall. There is a ritual about it, beginning with a wall and a knife. It communicates the road we are on. He is trapped, nowhere to run. He is pressed against the wall, and going to take any impact into his body, through it to the wall, and back again, driven in a second time. He is facing danger, sharp edges. He could be torn open. He is pressed against something rough and hard. He is still.

I am moving. He cannot see what's coming. My knife breaks the unspoken rules of knife play, and goes to places that feel forbidden and fraught with more danger than expected. And my knife shows my need. You can hear it in my breathing, feel it surge through my body. It travels the air in electric bursts of energy.

I play with it, toying with him, ramping my need up through his fear. I slap his face with the large blade. I run it along the top of his eye, just under the blindfold, teasing it against his eyelid, so he knows just how easy it would be to burst the eyeball. I fuck him with it, thrusting the tip under his jaw, not breaking skin, just teasing my cock to hardness at the thought of thrusting it deep. His breath is catching as I draw his lower lip down and slide the blade along it. My mouth swoops in out of nowhere and bites down on that lip, just barely breaking skin. This is a test of my control, as I slowly lick the fruit I have exposed, and growl deep in my throat.

He is hypnotically delicious, his blood electric in a way that is familiar and yet surprising. I grip his throat in my hand, constricting his breath, watching his face, his mouth. It is true. He has surprised me again. I tuck my new knowledge and my surprise away, knowing that I can do my worst. Folks always said that his kind make good boys for us. Perhaps I will be able to test that tonight. I release his throat and watch him breath deeply. I grip his hair and tilt his head back.

"Keep your mouth open and still."

I start to tease it in, watching the large black blade slide into his throat. I exhale loudly. He is motionless for me, breath held, taking my knife. My cock jumps at the sight, as I start to fuck his throat. Mine. This incredible wave of possessiveness roars through me as I thrust into him. And I want to see his eyes. I tear through the blindfold with my teeth, the blade still lodged in his throat, and meet his gaze. His eyes are shimmering, large, and full... full of what? I thrust in deeper, watching his pupils dilate with... is that joy? I can feel his heart race, see him struggle as he realizes he needs to breathe.

He must exercise perfect control, and not move his mouth or throat as he exhales and takes his first breath. Fear fills him. Not because he is afraid of the knife. Because he knows that it would displease me to draw blood when I don't intend to, and his whole being is focused on pleasing me. He works to do it perfectly, and contentment washes over his face as he succeeds. I thrust deeper in appreciation, picturing his throat muscles working to avoid contact with the blade. Oh this will be fun. I slide out of his throat.

I want my claws on his chest, now. I want to rip him open, expose him to my gaze, my teeth, my hunger. I want his blood on every tool in my possession. Now. I want to feast on him. I can feel the beast roll through my body.

Not yet. I want more pain to draw it out. I want to see if it's true. I want to know he can take my worst and still want more. I want to see his strength. That is worth delaying my feed. And postponing it will only make it sweeter.

I breathe deeply, focusing my senses as I walk slowly in front of him, inspecting him from every angle. He straightens his posture, easing into a position he can hold. I move close, and grip his shirt, tearing it swiftly from his chest and tossing it onto the floor. That's what I want first. I throw my shoulder into the body slam, and feel the electricity of our skins' contact. I trace my fingertips along the horizontal scars on his chest, and then grip his nipples, twisting. I am so close, I cannot resist sinking my teeth in and teasing myself. I bite deeply, barely avoiding breaking skin. Building connection. Making my cock throb. Drawing out my beast. I lift up and bite down, feeling his body shift with the pain, laying my mark on him. I claim him like this, first. Begin how you wish to proceed. With fear and pain and teeth and sex all rolled together. I can feel the blood pulsing just at the surface, calling me. I bite down hard and thrust my cock against him. My low growl mixes with the slow soft moan that escapes his lips. I lift my head to meet his eyes, and see that he has begun to fly.

I step back and begin my dance around him. Heaving my fist into his chest. My boot into his thigh. My open hand slamming down onto his pecs. I move rapidly, layering and shifting, gliding around him. Thrusting pain into him in unpredictable gusts of movement. Upping the ante. Ramming my boot into his cock, grinding the heel in and watching his eyes. He is twirling high in the air, lips parted, offering himself to me. His eyes entreat me to use him. And I do, exercising minute control, I coil into him, watching as he floats. This is just the beginning. I constrict his breath, cover his mouth and nose and thrust my teeth into his shoulder, feeling his heart against my tongue.

I lead him to the table and tell him to remove what he must to give me access to his ass. He takes off his pants and socks, folding them neatly and stacking them on top of his boots in the corner. He is wearing a simple leather jock. I order him face down onto the table. He is quivering. Mine, I think. And catch myself. I watch him, building on his fear, and remove my touch. There is only the knife sliding along him, forcing him to remain still. There is only the knife, as silence lays on him like a blanket. I step away, moving quietly, and leave him alone. We will see how much he needs connection, how much fear I can build. We will see, I think slowly to myself, how much distance I can tolerate.

My play is usually about connection. About driving myself inside. About opening someone up to my gaze. My tools are up close and personal. Play is my source of connection, and I usually hurl into it, deep and hard. I don't want to show myself yet. This must be done slowly. I want to see what he can do. I want to wait, before I commit myself to what I have already thought. I will come to that on my terms, in my time.

I collect my favorite canes, needing air between us. Needing that sound that whips through the air and blasts into flesh. Needing controlled, careful cruelty. Canes are a special love of mine. It takes a lot for me to risk thin sticks of wood, easily broken to form deadly weapons. Canes are about my risk, too. Their simple existence menaces. Their joy is unmatchable.

I line up my weapons on a nearby table, carefully. Thinking ahead, I select another item and place it on the table softly. I am ready.

I step back, allowing the necessary distance, and begin from stillness. I place my stripes precisely, just slow enough for him to get the full ripping effect of the bite. I lay lines of piercing sting, not holding back my strokes, saturating him with an invasive assault. There is nothing like the sound of a cane mutilating air, and he shivers at it. I can feel the fear rising off him like steam and breathe it in as my due.

I am unforgiving. It will never end. I can loom over him, layering slashes on skin, for eternity. I am breathing deeply. This is meditative. And I realize though there is air and space between us, I am attuned to his breathing. My cock swells at the almost imperceptible sounds he makes. We are connected. There is no breaking that. I know that he could be halfway across the country and I would feel the pulse of his blood. I smile at the thought, accepting it.

I am ready. Ready to rent his skin with my teeth and tools. To break him open and take a good long taste. To unleash the beast roaming in my skin.

I feel an incredible calm at the roaring in my blood. A new calm. I can fully be who I am in this room, with this man. He is strong enough. And I trust him enough to risk. I pick up my belt, and begin.

There are few tools I have a deeper connection with. I have had this belt since the 19th century, and cared for it well. It is a part of me. An extension of my cock and my will. Nothing brings out my beast like my belt. Which is why I keep it at home, and only use it on prey I am going to devour. Until now.

I explain this to him, watching him tremble.

"Please use me, Sir," is all he says.

Mine. I double the belt and start slamming him with it, the welts rising rapidly. Vision begins to blur. This is all about sound and movement. My body senses where to strike. My blows hammer him into the table. I can feel a growl building in my throat as his scent shifts. My cock swells, as I hurl the belt into his back in rapid crashing surges.

"Mine," I growl. "Mine to hurt. Mine to use. Mine to feed on. Mine."

The possessiveness rises in me, a tsunami cresting and breaking over him as I blast the belt into his back, rending his skin. Welts form on top of welts, and break the surface. He is moaning as I howl, the beast fully in my skin and oh so hungry. I lay the belt across the back of his neck and crouch on the table above him, eyes focused on the gashes opening his back to me. I drop on top of him, rubbing my chest into the blood on his back.

I breathe the scent of him in and growl happily, "Mine."

I free my cock, swollen to bursting, and shed my pants. I will savor the first real taste. Right now, it's enough to smell it and feel it against my skin, and know there is more for the taking. I rub it onto my cock, stroking it in as I close my eyes. I want inside, now. Want to rend him open. Thrust myself into him, bloody and hard. I want to tear his back open with claws and teeth, and feast.

I describe this to him, and he moans his consent.

"Please, Sir," he says softly. "Please."

He is all want and need and craving, and where his hunger meets mine we will crest. Mine. The word fills me, taking me over.

I thrust into him, my cock smeared in his blood, ramming into his ass for my pleasure. He is so open for me, so willing. His groans are loud and true as I fuck him, rubbing my face in the blood on his back. I grip his hips, and stop, embedded in him. I can feel my claws extend right before I slash into his back, ripping him open. The blood flows freely and I bathe my chest in it, bellowing as I hurl my cock into him. I wrap the belt around his neck, constricting his breath, my cock pounding him into the table, and I bite. Mulled wine. Spicy. Sweet. Tangy. I drink him down, savoring each gulp, thrusting steadily. I release his neck, hear his gasping breaths, and bite harder, feeding.

"Please, Sir," he manages in a throaty whisper.

I lift my head. "Please what, boy?"

This is the first time I have called him boy, and he whimpers at the sound of it.

"Please, Sir. Please may I cum, Sir?"

I thrust into him hard, and feel his ass grab me.

"Mine. You are my boy. Mine to fuck. Mine to slash open. Mine to devour. Mine to mark. Mine to command. You may cum when I sink my teeth into you again, boy. I want to hear it. Tell me you are mine, and then you may cum."

I drive my cock into him, reaming him deeply, and rub my chest against his bloody back. I reach around to grab his cock, gripping it tightly and stroking it in quick bursts. I plunge my teeth into his shoulder. Gnawing him open. Snarling as I drink. My dick pumping into him.

"I am yours, Sir. I offer myself freely for your use. I am so glad to be yours, Sir."

I explode into him, storms crashing in huge tidal waves. Drinking and cumming. Releasing myself and drawing him in. His ass clenches around me in spasms as he bursts, his body bucking and shuddering.

I continue to feed. When his body calms, I am sated, and I ease myself out of him slowly. I take my time licking his wounds closed, savoring the taste of him. I pull him up into my arms, smiling.

"Now let's see that cock of yours, boy."

His eyes go wide, he looks down and he starts trembling again. I lift his chin to meet his eyes, and then trace the scars on his chest lightly with my tongue. I lift my head to stare into his eyes again, and slowly unzip the jock, revealing a large black silicone cock. I pump it hard, stroking it against him, where I know he is enlarged by testosterone.

"Did you think I didn't know, boy? After all the centuries I've lived, did you think I did not learn how to read people?"

I grin into his eyes.

"You are my boy. And I am proud to claim you as mine."

I gather him to me, holding him tight, and start imagining possibilities.

* * * *

Kiss & Make Up
© Ashley Lister

"According to Descartes," Dracula began slowly, "I think, therefore I am. However, if I think I am a vampire, and we accept that vampires don't exist, does this mean that I don't exist?"

Bob and Linda exchanged a glance.

"What's wrong with him tonight?" asked Bob.

Linda rolled her eyes and shook her head. She cut a striking figure striding by his side. She was tall and raven-haired and dressed in a clinging suit comprised of black leather jeans with a matching jacket. Her skin was as white as alabaster except for the full, ripe lips that hid her elongated canines. Bob noticed that Linda's ample chest rose and fell swiftly, as it always did after she had fed. Her long, scarlet nails glinted with slivers of silver moonlight as her fingers twitched impatiently by her hips.

"It's Dracula's dark gift," Linda explained. "Whoever he's been feeding from, he temporarily absorbs some aspect of their personality. When he feeds from drunks, he acts drunk. When he feeds from stoners he gets high." She tossed an impatient glance in Dracula's direction and added, "This is what he gets like after feeding on philosophy students. He'll spend the night being metaphysical and talking incomprehensible bullshit."

Bob nodded and accepted this. He had been feeling a little light-headed himself since feeding and he suspected it was because his victim had been a student.

It had been his idea to visit the Student Union bar.

Admittedly the necks weren't particularly clean, and most of the victims contained more chemicals than an overstocked pharmacist, but the feeding had been easy, quick and ultimately satisfying. Now, with his bloodlust sated, Bob found his thoughts were moving to different yet more familiar appetites. Staring hungrily at Linda, he licked his lips and graced her with an appreciative smile.

"You've been with Dracula for a while?"

"We've been partners for a couple of centuries," Linda allowed. "Although there are times when it feels longer. Sometimes I think we're just staying together so we can piss each other off and then kiss and make up."

Bob nodded as though he understood. He didn't understand, but he wanted Linda to consider him a good listener so the pretence was essential. He'd read somewhere that women appreciated men who were good listeners and earning Linda's approval was an all-consuming goal that seemed more important than ever now he had fed.

"Dracula doesn't strike me as the most attentive partner," Bob ventured.

Linda shot a scornful glare in Dracula's direction. The legendary vampire was studying the back of his hand with an expression of dappy amazement on his face. His violet eyes were wide and incredulous. His lips silently formed the word, "Wow!"

"He's been doing this sort of thing for a long time," Linda sighed. She gestured back toward the cemetery gates, and Bob got the idea she was indicating the carnage they had left behind at the Student Union bar. Linda's voice was tinged with a mixture of sadness and frustration. "There are times when Dracula forgets that feeding can fuel urges in some of us younger vampires."

"Urges?"

Linda glanced at him. Her eyes were as violet and expressive as Dracula's and they glistened with encouragement. "Strong urges," she murmured.

The trio continued walking through the cemetery. It was a convenient shortcut back to the house they were using as a temporary refuge for their mini-coven. The route was also an apposite reminder of the death they had caused during their feeding frenzy at the SU. Whilst Dracula paused and marveled over the "awesome" lichen moss he had found on one ancient headstone, Bob and Linda continued to walk briskly through the moonlit necropolis. Bob noticed that Dracula was falling behind but he kept the observation to himself as he and Linda crunched their way down the gravel path.

"So, feeding fuels strong urges in you?" he prompted.

"Feeding fuels strong urges in *all* us younger vampires," Linda assured him. Her voice had fallen to a husky drawl. "All that biting, feeding and intimacy. Touching strange human flesh. Penetrating bare skin. Tasting blood." She shivered. Her eyes shone. "It's like an appetizer before a meal," she explained. "*Or like foreplay.*"

Bob paused before responding, not sure he could speak without nervousness trembling in his voice. He regarded Linda with solemn appreciation and said, "What's the point of an appetizer if there's no main course to follow?"

"Exactly."

"And what's the point of foreplay if there's no..."

"Exactly," she said again.

With a small giggle Linda snatched at his hand and dragged him away from the cemetery path. The action was so swift that Bob was briefly unsure what was happening. Their feet gave a final scrunch on the gravel before Bob found Linda had led him to a patch of moist grass. She pulled him down into the discreet shelter behind a tall tombstone. Stretching out on the grass, she arranged herself beneath him with her legs spread wide apart so he could comfortably kneel between them. His body was pressed firmly against hers. The position was so intimate he could feel himself immediately growing hard.

His erection throbbed with the sudden prospect of pleasure.

Since he'd become a vampire his senses seemed more highly attuned. He was aware of the faraway sound of Dracula stumbling along the gravel path; the distant chirrup of nocturnal insects and birds calling to each other in the night; and the closer scent of Linda's sexual hunger. For an instant he could picture her thoughts, an ability he had come to think of as his own dark gift. In Linda's mind he could see they were both already naked, their pallid bodies entwined beneath moonlight on the graveyard grass, and his erection was plunging slowly and solidly into the yielding split of her sex. It was a powerful image and he shut it from his thoughts before Linda could realize he had been reading her mind.

"You do have strong urges, don't you?" he muttered.

"I think we both have strong urges."

She was tugging at the belt that fastened his jeans. For any other woman her long fingernails would have made the task awkward and cumbersome. Linda slipped the belt open with practiced ease and then began to work on the buttons of his jeans, popping them apart with casual dexterity.

"I think we have the same strong urges," Linda assured him. "And I think we both know how to sate them."

He placed his hand on her wrist, momentarily stopping her from releasing the last of the buttons. "Are you sure this is wise?"

"Don't you want to do this?"

He laughed, keeping the sound muted for fear of alerting Dracula to the whereabouts of their hiding place. "I didn't mean that. You know I want to do this as much as you do, but..." He glanced over his shoulder and peered past the shelter of the gravestone.

Dracula continued to stumble down the gravel path. He was now walking with his head held back as he stared at the stars in the sky above. The ancient vampire's face was a mask of childish wonderment. Slowly, he murmured the words, "That is so fucking awesome."

"I mean," Bob told Linda, "What about him? Won't he be pissed off if he catches us together?"

"Damn right he'd be pissed off," Linda agreed. "He'd be absolutely livid." In a conspiratorial whisper that tickled against his earlobe she added, "So we'd best make sure he doesn't catch us." Moving her face from Bob's ear, she placed a kiss against his mouth and slid her tongue between his lips.

Bob made no further attempt to resist. He moved his hand from Linda's wrist and allowed her to kiss him with ferocious hunger whilst her fingers slipped easily into his jeans. Her hands were icy cold—partly from the night's chill and partly because Linda was all vampire. The cool touch of her fingers against his erection was enough to make him yearn for her with a fresh and furious desire. When her hand encircled his shaft, he had to pull his mouth away from her kiss for fear of losing control from the excitement.

"You do have some strong urges, don't you?" Linda whispered.

"As strong as yours," he countered.

Linda's jacket was fastened by a zipper. He pulled it open in one fluid movement to reveal the bare skin beneath. Shadows and darkness kept her body briefly from his view but he traced his hands over the exposed flesh, blindly reveling in the sensation of caressing her naked body.

Linda moaned.

Bob pushed his mouth over Linda's. In an instant the pair were embroiled in a passionate, sultry kiss. As their lips connected, and their tongues wrestled and battled with hungry eagerness, Bob could feel his need for Linda growing more urgent and desperate.

His fingertips brushed over the hard thrust of one nipple.

A spark of electric excitement crackled from his touch. "Fuck! Yes!"

Encouraged, Bob caught the stiff bead of flesh and teased it firmly between finger and thumb.

The effect on Linda was immediate. She writhed wantonly beneath him. Holding her breast still, so Bob could continue to tease her, she tore at his clothes with animal fury. His shirt was shredded and then wrenched away. Then his jeans were ripped open and tugged downward.

Equally eager to experience Linda's completely bare body, Bob stripped the jacket from her ultra-white torso. Because they had shifted positions slightly he was afforded his first glimpse of her naked breasts. The sight of her full bosom made his erection throb with renewed urgency. The tips of her nipples were thick and rigid. They flushed cherry red against her moonlight pale skin. Unable to resist, Bob lowered his mouth to one breast and sucked hungrily.

Linda stiffened and then her loins rose up to meet him. Her body pulsated against his as though they were already in the throes of a more passionate and penetrative act. As Bob greedily sucked and slurped against her nipple he could feel the woman beneath him responding eagerly.

"Fuck me! I want you to fuck me." Her hand returned to his erection and she gripped it with a force that was almost agonizing. "I want you to fuck me now and fuck me hard," she panted. "Do it, Bob."

Bob grinned and began to slowly peel the leather jeans from her hips. If Linda was desperate for him now, he felt sure she would be insane with desire by the time he had slipped the jeans from her legs.

"Quickly," she insisted.

Bob whispered his response whilst planting lazy kisses against her bare thighs. "I'm going as quick as I can."

"Linda!"

Dracula's plaintive voice echoed from the darkness. He sounded far away, but not so far away that Bob thought they could consider themselves safe.

"Hey! Linda!" Dracula called. "Where've you gone, hon? I think I'm lost again."

"Keep quiet," Linda gasped.

Bob hadn't needed the warning. He had no intention of letting Dracula know where they were or what they were doing. He didn't make a sound but simply continued to ease the leather jeans down Linda's muscular thighs and plant the occasional kiss against her freshly exposed skin. The scent of her sex had already reached his nostrils. The fragrance of animal need—wet and ready for him—was so irresistible he could think of nothing except devouring her. He finally pulled the jeans from her legs and then lowered his face to Linda's moist split. Like a connoisseur he marveled briefly over the beauty of her appearance and then gently inhaled her fragrance.

Her natural perfume was intoxicating.

His erection throbbed again and he realized if he simply continued to drink in the scent of her pussy, he could possibly reach his climax from that stimulus alone. When he finally lowered his mouth, stroking his tongue against Linda's moist lips, an orgasmic rush of bliss bristled through his body.

"Fuck!" Linda groaned. "That's good."

"Yes," Bob agreed. He stroked his tongue against her lips again, savoring her rich musk as it tormented his senses.

"Linda!" Dracula called. "Where the hell are you, Linda? I'm getting pissed now."

To Bob, Dracula's distant cries were as meaningless as the night's chill or the collection of freshly drained corpses they had left behind at the SU bar. All that existed for him were Linda's words of encouragement and the sweet flavor of her sex against his tongue. He teased the lips of her labia apart and trilled the tip of his tongue against her pulsing clitoris. Then he pushed his tongue between her pussy lips, enjoying the sensation of her inner muscles as they clenched sporadically against him. Her responsiveness was a further joy. As Linda trembled beneath him and urged him to continue, Bob couldn't recall a moment when his arousal had felt so powerful or so satisfying.

"Aw! Come on, Linda," Dracula called. "Don't tell me you've gone off screwing that new kid? I thought you said you were done fooling around after I ripped the viscera out of that last one of your conquests?"

Bob slowly pulled his head away from Linda's pussy. His lower jaw glistened with the sheen of her arousal. Linda must have seen he was unsettled because she placed a reassuring hand on his chest and shook her head. In the softest whisper she said, "Don't listen to him. Dracula didn't rip out anyone's viscera. He's just saying that to try and make himself sound scary."

Bob didn't want to tell Linda that Dracula had succeeded in making himself sound scary. Such an admission was likely to make him appear undesirable and he didn't want to do anything that would spoil the chance of sharing his climax with Linda. Accepting her reassurance, and spurred on by the fact that she was now guiding his erection to her open sex, he forced himself to push his length between her thighs.

There was an instant of pure bliss.

The un-vampiric heat of her sex was a furnace around his icy shaft. Her inner muscles gripped his length more tightly than Linda had managed with her strong, powerful hands. As he slid deeper, his length lubricated by a meld of his own saliva and Linda's copious juices, Bob could feel the climax building in his loins.

Linda pressed her mouth close to Bob's ear and said, "Don't let Dracula worry you with all that talk about ripping out a guy's viscera. It's not true."

Bob was past caring. Sliding in and out of her moist, velvety warmth, he slowed his rhythm so that it matched Linda's steady and relentless motion. His thoughts were occupied only with the divine sensations around his shaft and the determination to stretch their shared pleasure for as long as possible.

Linda shivered beneath him. She jammed a fist into her mouth at one point to stifle a scream of satisfaction. Bob could feel the flood of fresh warm moisture soaking his length as he continued to plough in and out of her sex. When she nibbled lightly on his ear and said, "Fill me with your cum," he finally allowed himself the release his body craved.

His length sputtered and pulsed.

A rush of orgasmic relief flooded his body.

Beneath him, Linda groaned with soft satisfaction. She continued to ride her pussy against his pulsing length, milking every last drop of the seed from him and shivering as though his release had been as satisfying for her as it had been for him.

"Linda!" Dracula exclaimed.

Bob stiffened. Cold fingers grabbed his shoulder and then he was torn away from Linda and thrown against a headstone. He caught a brief glimpse of Linda, naked on the grass, her legs spread and a white trickle of his seed dribbling from the spread lips of her sex. And then Dracula was standing over him and fixing him with the most menacing scowl.

"I'll rip your viscera out!" Dracula bellowed.

Linda was struggling to find her clothes. "Don't worry about his empty threats. I told you: he never ripped out anyone's viscera. He's never done that to any of the guys I've played with. All Dracula's ever done was make me help him to suck every last drop of blood from the body of the guy I'd been fooling with."

Dracula turned to glare at her.

Bob saw that Dracula's glare became a smile of approval. He was devastated to see Linda return the smile to her partner.

"It's almost like one of those bonding exercise they make couples do in marriage counseling," Linda said sweetly. She was talking to Bob but staring directly at Dracula. "I think it allowed us to redevelop our trust for one another again." Her voice had a dreamy quality. "It was like we'd had a chance to kiss and make up. And it was so sexual!"

"And the guy you were both sucking?" Bob broke in.

Linda shrugged as though the matter was of no consequence. "Just another dead vampire. No creature can survive without having some blood coursing through its veins. Vampires are no exception to that rule."

Dracula grinned and dragged Bob from the floor. "She's right," he confirmed. "No creature can survive without having some blood coursing through its veins." His grin grew menacing as he added, "And you're about to find out just how true that is."

* * * *

Afterwards, back in the house they were using as temporary refuge, with Bob's drained remains a rotting memory in the graveyard, Dracula turned to Linda and smiled. His lips remained crimson, moist and sultry. "You're going to think I'm depraved," he started. "But, ever since we drained Bob, I've been getting urges." He laughed self-consciously and said, "Does that sound depraved to you?"

Linda shook her head. "It doesn't sound depraved. It simply sounds like you're making the most of your dark gift."

He beckoned her with a finger. "Want to help me make the most of my dark gift?"

Linda shook her head. "I'd love to help," she admitted. "But I need to go out before sunrise and recruit a new member for our mini-coven."

A flash of annoyance furrowed his brow. "Already? Can't we go one night without having a third member in our group?" Fixing her with an accusatory glower, he added, "And are you going to fuck this one too?"

She brushed up against him and laughed. "Of course I am," she purred. "If I don't do something to piss you off, you and I won't have any reason to reconcile, will we?" Her fingers brushed against the swell of his thickening erection as she added, "And we both know how much fun it is when we have the chance to kiss and make up."

* * * *

Devouring Heart
© Andrea Dale

The music throbbed, a heavy beat that spoke of dark things. Dark things that, like the music, got under your breastbone and lodged there, pressing rhythmically against your heart. Most of the lights in the club were red, making everyone look as though they had been doused with fresh blood.

It was like being inside a pulsating heart. I moved through it, aorta and ventricle and life-affirming beats, looking for Sorcha.

Sorcha first walked into the club two years ago. I remember the night, of course. Everyone turned to stare, because she was gorgeous.

Straight, blue-streaked black hair down to her ass. Said ass was delectable, covered in a leather miniskirt over ripped fishnets. She wore a white baby-doll top that depicted a mouth biting into a broken heart. The shirt was skintight, at least a size too small. It revealed a slice of pouty tummy and outlined a pair of pierced nipples.

I wanted nothing more than to rub my own breasts against those cold rings, to wrap my hands around her tight ass and grind my crotch against hers until we were both screaming incoherently.

But first, I wanted to ask her to dance.

I didn't believe in love at first sight. I'm still not sure I do, not even now. It took me a couple of months to fall in love with her, or so I tell myself. That first night, however, when she walked in, and everybody stared, and everybody wanted her...it didn't matter.

She walked straight up to me.

Dancing was just exquisite, excruciating foreplay for both of us. After two or three songs, her pierced tongue was licking my earlobe in time to the driving beat of the music, making me imagine what that would feel like against my clit, which pulsed in the same rhythm. Her hands reminded me that my belly ring made that area a huge erogenous zone for me.

I soared and swam in a sea of scarlet desire.

I took her home that night, and fulfilled those fantasies I was having and then some. Playing with her nipple piercings was enough to make her come, and we discovered her hands were small enough to fit inside of me. When she uncurled her fist in my slippery cunt, my vision bloomed roses, red and black.

I'd had my share of one-night stands, and I told myself I didn't expect her to be much more than that. I'd be happy if she stuck around, but I didn't dare hope for it. At the end of the night, she told me she loved me. When I asked her how that was possible, she said, "I didn't know I was looking for anyone, but when I walked in and I saw you, I just *knew*."

Two years later, it was my turn to walk in looking for her. Because five days ago, she'd disappeared.

I didn't see her anywhere, but it was hard to see anything at all through the crush of dancing bodies. I mounted the industrial metal steps up to the bar, where I'd have a better view.

Ambrose, looking dashing as usual in a tuxedo top made out of strips of black and white leather with a bowtie of spikes, handed me a double shot of vodka before I asked. I drank it in one gulp, without a shudder. I couldn't taste anything these days.

"I'm sorry, Case, but you missed her," he said. "She left maybe half an hour ago."

I nodded my thanks to him, paid double what I owed, and left. Outside, I threw the shot glass against the wall, but the sound of shattering glass didn't help. Then I went to Sorcha's house.

She hadn't bothered to lock the front door. Not that I couldn't have picked the lock if that had been necessary. I'd done it before, these past five days, to find the place empty. I'd even waited inside all one night, creeping out just before dawn.

If my actions screamed "stalker!" or "crazed ex-lover!" I didn't fucking care, okay? Maybe even crazy stalkers think they have their reasons, think it's all is for the best.

They were in the bedroom, and from the moans of ecstasy, I assumed they were having sex. No reason not to, I supposed. I flipped on the light. Sorcha favored blue bulbs, and it was like peering through a bottle of Curacao, or swimming in a Caribbean sea (not that I'd ever see that). She was wearing the sapphire satin corset I'd bought her. My gut wrenched, ached more than I expected it to.

Her partner's head shot up, but Sorcha was slower to move, languidly disengaging her teeth from the other woman's wrist.

"Case," she said. She sounded drunk. That's the sensation vampires feel when they're feeding. I'd guessed what had happened to her when she disappeared, and Ambrose had confirmed my suspicions three days ago. If you hang out long enough at the club, you'll get approached with an offer. Not everybody takes it, and I was surprised—stunned—that Sorcha had.

I grabbed the other woman—whose mouth was blood-wet, so I knew she'd already fed—and threw her at the bedroom door. The jamb splintered when she slammed against it.

"Get the fuck out," I snarled. She pulled herself upright and snarled incoherently back, but she left. I heard the front door bang shut.

"Case," Sorcha said again.

"Sorcha, you idiot," I said, kneeling on the bed next to her. "Why didn't you tell me?"

"I was afraid, Case," she said, and I heard the desperation in her voice. "I didn't want—I don't want—"

"Never mind," I said, still with a snarl in my voice. "Just shut up and fuck me."

Our coupling was as violent and incredible as our first. I yanked her sweet breasts out from the corset before she knew what hit her, and I straddled her thigh and used the nipple rings like reins. I rode her, but in truth I wasn't after my own gratification—not yet, at least.

Did I want to punish her for running away from me? Maybe, a little. Punishment for Sorcha was pleasure, so it wasn't as if I was teaching her a lesson.

I couldn't deny her. My knee wedged between her legs but it almost wasn't needed, because she could come just from the way I twisted and tugged the piercings. Her nipples flushed near-purple, and she bucked beneath me, writhing in pain that transmuted into pleasure and back again.

"It's okay," I whispered, my lips pressed against the pulse in her neck.

After that first round of orgasms she had recovered from the feeding and was stronger, so I let her take control. ("It's okay," she'd whispered back, and I'd believed her.) She buckled leather cuffs—blue, like her corset—around my wrists. The cheap gold spray paint had worn away from the wooden headboard wood where the cuffs had been chained time and time again.

Then she strapped on our favorite black dildo and thrust it towards my mouth. Black dildo, blue satin, blurring into a bruise as I sucked. She knew what I wanted, what I would have begged for if she hadn't been gagging me with the silicone cock, and that was to have it inside me. To have her leaning over me, sweaty and flushed, while she plunged it into me.

But even when she did, she teased and toyed—and restrained, I could do nothing but force my hips harder toward hers, struggling for satisfaction. It wasn't our usual game, but I was so happy to have found her again that even the frustration was mixed with a contradictory sense of relief.

Still, when she pulled the dildo out of me, I swore at her. Nasty terms of endearment. She smiled, just a little, as she promised me what I'm begging for.

She slid a smaller vibrating cock into my ass and slid her face down my body, I assumed to lick my aching clit. Instead she tongued my belly piercing, and I arched my back as best I could. That's when she pressed another vibrator to my clit. Then all I knew was that I shattered and screamed and ultimately came very, very close to passing out. When I thought I couldn't bear to come anymore, I begged her to stop, insisting I would die even though we both knew that couldn't happen.

She undid one of the cuffs so I could tuck my arm around her before she fell asleep on my chest. Exhausted, sated, finally back in her embrace, I followed her into oblivion.

Which shows just how irrationally desperate I am for a happy ending. As always, I should have known better.

* * * *

I woke to the sandpaper rasp of teeth scraping my neck. I sighed my contentment; so this is what she wanted, after all.

But she'd barely broken the skin before she pulled away, sobbing.

"Sorcha?" I reached out my free hand.

"I'm sorry, Case, but I can't do it. I can't bring you down into this. I know it sounds like the perfect life: never aging, never dying, feasting in the dark." She gave a bark of humorless laughter. "The perfect goth fantasy. But it's not. The killing makes me sick. The drinking is...abhorrent to me. It's disgusting. I can't make you do that, too. I love you, and I want you with me always, but I can't let you suffer with me."

She ran out of the bedroom. A moment later, I saw the bright crack of light between the heavy curtains, and realized it was full morning.

"Sorcha, no!"

I wrenched at the cuff, now a prison, until I heard the headboard crack and splinter. I was halfway down the stairs when Sorcha opened the door. I screamed her name again, and she turned.

"I love you," she said, stepped backwards into the sunlight, and died.

* * * *

I spent the rest of the day in her house, trapped. I lost count of how many times I walked up to that open door and stood there, looking out.

I'd known what had happened to her in those five missing days, and I'd allowed the same thing to happen to me, so we could be together always.

She never gave me the chance to tell her.

But I can't bring myself to step outside. Sorcha, in the end, was far braver than I can ever be.

* * * *

71

Blood Tint
© Raziel Moore

"Relax, Alak. Nothing's going to bite you."

Daci's words were old and familiar, repeated countless times as we'd begun evening walks. And, as always, her words brought comfort. I took a deep breath, and held tight to the arm she interlocked with mine.

"I know, I know." Another familiar refrain. I could let Daciana walk the sunset alone, just like she could let me go by myself in the pre-dawn. But we don't. Each for the other, a gift we give every day we can. I admit that, in this part of the world, the reds of sunset are often richer and more long lasting than the blush of dawn.

The sun had just set and the sky glowed crimson. I was my agitated dusk self, still wearing my sunglasses as we walked along the Soho street. Spring was definitely coming, and we'd already begun to discuss going south, but were undecided about the muggy equator or winter in Christchurch or Johannesburg. We had a week or two left to think about it, but an early blow of warm weather following the last major gales of March made New York feel, for a brief moment, like a city of much lower latitude—close and steamy. The restaurants and galleries took notice, seizing the opportunity to throw open their doors and waft cooking smells and music and light into the puddled street. We weren't terribly hungry. Soon, though.

Daci and I weren't headed anywhere in particular, allowing our feet to guide us where they might. She's more solicitous toward me as the winter ebbs, and the sun keeps eating further into the night. There was a good jazz club a few blocks down, and I had half a mind to pass the evening there. It was a good place for finding—

My thoughts were interrupted.

"Daci?"

She stood frozen in midstride, pale face upturned. Her eyes and mouth were closed, but the rise and fall of her petite chest told me she was sniffing the air intently.

"Mmm. I smell something. Something delicious." The tone of her voice certainly caught my attention, as did the flush on her face. She wasn't talking about restaurants or bakeries.

Her nose is so much more sensitive than mine, especially when I'm not hunting, that I know better than to question it.

"Where?" I asked, and Daci nodded—diagonally across the street. The bright, clean lights of a gallery spilled out of the plate glass window and open door. Dirty jazz and the sound of people. A show opening.

"Shall we go see?"

She nodded and, still arm in arm, we crossed Mercer street. Daci's gait changed as she moved, becoming more fluid and swaying. Predatory. I couldn't help but catch her excitement.

The entrance to The Recombined Gallery opened into a spacious single room display area, with partition walls that didn't go all the way to the ceiling carving up the space. The artist on exhibit was a crossbreed pop-art painter/sculptor whose work I'd not encountered before. This seemed like his first big show—or else he'd found a magnanimous patron. Plentiful hors d'oeuvres and wine circulated, even for people just off the street.

The fortuitous passage of a server allowed me to snag a pair of glasses at the door. I took a sniff and guessed at a Finger Lakes red. As I handed one to Daci, it was my turn to stop in my tracks.

A painting—a portrait, clearly not by the show's main attraction—held a semi-prominent place just to the side of the entrance, under a sign reading "Next Opening, April 14". The painting itself was gorgeous: the subject, a man of indeterminate age, painted in bold, dirty strokes in a palette of grays, blacks and rusty reds. That color—

"Oh, my."

"Yes, this is it, Alak."

I knew she was right. I had at last caught the scent at the doorway myself, but it was much stronger here. The reddish tints in the portrait...they were, at least in part, dried blood. Even desiccated and dead, like a pressed flower, the lingering scent of it spoke of something surpassing. This close, the inescapable scent brought with it an unbidden, early hunger. My fangs wanted to descend of their own accord, as if I could drink the painting itself.

I caught Daci laughing quietly to herself.

"You know, the face looks a little like you."

"I bet you say that to all the boys," I snorted, but, looking again, I had to admit she wasn't entirely wrong.

"Do you think it's the artist's blood?" I asked.

"Good question. Artists are an odd lot."

My mouth twitched at the old joke, and I decided not to mention any of our many creative flirtations. "Perhaps we should find the artist and ask."

"Oh, I bet she's here."

"She?" Daci's sense of smell is so good that—

"She," she said, pointing at the sign under the painting. "Neave Flynn".

"Huh." *I'm* supposed to be the one with the better eyesight, dammit. I blamed it on the painting's distracting media, and began scanning the gallery crowd as Daci sniffed the air and nodded, a grin teasing at her lips.

"The living source is somewhere close—artist or not. The painting is stale by comparison. I'm sure I can sniff it out. Even in this crowd, the sweetness should be like a beacon... Alak?"

74

"Yes?"

"What have *you* found?"

Maybe it was the instigation of the painting, but my senses were all coming alive now, and my eyes had picked this one out like rose among lilies. I moved to stand behind Daciana, nosing a lock of blonde hair behind her ear and pointing with a hand resting on her shoulder.

"Do you see her, Daci?"

She turned away from the painting and cocked her head to one side, scanning the milling arts crowd for a moment, then nodded.

"Ah, yes," she purred. "You do have an eye, Alak. She looks divine."

She settled her frame back against me as we both watched the crimson-clad woman navigate the far side of the room. Dark brown hair swept across her shoulders as she conversed with a man in a blazer and turtleneck, her full breasts nearly spilling from her frock, but not quite. Everything about her was alive. And the way she canted her round hips, and placed her hand on the man's while she laughed at his words was not quite simple flirtation.

"She's hunting," Daci said.

"Seems so. And she's good at it."

"In her own way."

"Do you think she would want to catch me?"

Daci chuckled again. "So you're going to play and leave me to hunt for our artist?"

"You are the lioness, Daci."

"And you are what, a gazelle?"

"Sometimes. When I choose to be."

Daci snorted. Very unladylike. "Yes. I think she will be happy to hunt you. She may not like what she catches, though."

"Oh, you know she will. One way or the other."

75

I left a glistening trail of saliva behind Daci's ear and stepped away, winding through the crowd I moved past patrons ogling acrylic-and-metal canvases of mundane and clever design. The lighting was that infernal new natural spectrum type, so I kept my sunglasses on. In this crowd, I was right in style.

There was no shortage of very pretty people here, men and women, some with scents or presences that would have been interesting and entertaining on another day. Tonight, I passed them by.

My quarry had spun herself away from her turtle-necked friend and wound a path between patrons, kissing women's cheeks and smiling demurely at the proffered masculine hands. It was easy to put myself in her path and pretend to examine a brass sculpture—a cross between a can-opener and a brassiere. I turned to move on to the next piece just as she swept from a chatty exchange with the septuagenarian art critic from *The Voice*.

The collision was brief, her dark tresses swinging against my open collar as we rebounded. I allowed the force to splash a drop or two of wine onto my hand.

"Oh dear, I'm terribly sorry."

Irish, South coast. Away five years or less...

She grabbed from a nearby server. "Not at all, very clumsy of me, I—"

I stopped mid-sentence, though, as she handed me the napkin and our fingers brushed. For some reason, I was almost dangerously slow tonight. I found myself staring at her for a moment, something I never do.

"Are you all right?" she asked with quirked smile. Her face showed genuine concern; I must have looked quite rattled. It wasn't an act, either. In close proximity, her beauty fulfilled the promise of the distant view, but more than that. She reached out to touch my arm and the contact was electric. All my senses jumped.

"Oh, quite all right, thank you. You know, and I'm sure you hear this often, but you look familiar to me, though I'm also sure we haven't met before."

Her smile was like a remembered flash of sunshine, but without the pain.

"Yes, I get that a lot, both honestly and as a pickup line. Which was that?"

Bold and challenging. Looking to see the reaction of someone she was calling out. I laughed, easing into the game.

"Both, honestly. But I have much better lines. I only used that one because it was true. Truth has real benefits."

She nodded, frankly assessing me. In her low-rise heels, she didn't have to look up much to meet my eyes. "I bet *you* don't get that line very often," she said.

I chuckled again. "No, not here. In that you're quite right."

"Which may make it seem odd that I have the same feeling."

"Oh?" I extended my hand, "Well, let us try to remember each other better, then. My name is Alak."

After a pause, she shook my hand.

"Neave" she said, and, though the first scent of her up close had given it away, a thrill went through me. I brought her hand to my lips for a kiss, and the scent of her blood welled through her skin. As my lips grazed the back of her hand, I inhaled deeply, surreptitiously, and let the kiss linger a heartbeat or two longer than appropriate for a first introduction.

I heard her breath catch, and felt the tension race up her arm to her hand. She almost jerked it away, but didn't.

When I looked up, a faint blush colored her cheeks. My fangs had emerged fully of their own accord, and I kept my own smile close-lipped until I could reassert control. I had thrown her off her hunt. But she'd thrown me off mine, so we were even, as it went. I had to show her to Daci.

"Neave," I said. "Neave Flynn?"

She nodded.

"That's your portrait by the door? Your show is coming up, yes?"

She smiled. She knew I knew the answer. We'd started the dance. I hadn't let go of her hand.

"It is exquisite. Your style is completely different from the current artist's."

"We shared a studio until last year. Paul helped me swing my own show"

"Good friends are like jewels."

"He'd call that horribly bourgeois," she laughed, "but Paul's a good guy."

We made our way through the gallery. "And now you have your own space?"

"Yes, half a loft, not too far from here. And you?"

"Oh, I stay usually a bit more toward the park."

"So you're just visiting the city?"

"Yes, but I come regularly."

We both knew how this went, hinting without telling too much, teasing without revealing. She played it well, but then so did I. And while she had already caught me from first sight, it was becoming mutual. And it wasn't just my dashing charm either. I was doing surprisingly little. There was something else in her—rawer, more instinctive than socialite games.

When we arrived back at her painting, Daci was still there— or, more likely, back from her own circulation. I was certain she'd picked Neave's scent up much earlier. In fact, I now wondered if Daci had made the connection when I first pointed Neave out, but had let me discover her for myself. When I introduced them, Daci smiled broadly and, instead of an air kiss, took the back of Neave's hand to her own lips. As I had done, she inhaled the woman's scent and glowed with it. A glance showed me how pleased she was.

Neave raised an eyebrow at this new wrinkle. That I had arrived with a companion wasn't necessarily unusual, but Daci's kiss disconcerted her. The game was a little different than she'd thought. Actually, it was a lot different, but everything in its time. Seeing Neave close up, Daci was just as taken with her as I was, though she, as always, exhibited just a bit more control than I ever could. Her teeth betrayed no hint in her broad smile.

"And so this dark, brooding man is yours?" Daci asked Neave, pointing to the painting, but facing me.

"Oh, no! Well yes, sort of, he's mine in that I thought of him. I didn't use a model. I usually don't."

"And how do you fix the blood so it doesn't decay?"

Neave jerked her hand from Daci's with a short gasp and looked around, as if to check if Daci could be overheard.

"Blood? What makes you say that? What do you mean?"

"Oh, come now, dear, it's quite obvious. There is a textural quality you simply cannot get any other way."

Now Daci was playing. My eye could discern that kind of detail, but hers couldn't.

"I... I use a dilution in the red, and a little... It's not... You won't..."

"Tell anyone? Not at all. We wouldn't dream of it. Please, we have no interest in playing police or holding any secrets over your head."

79

She didn't seem much relieved. We'd seen straight through a personal mystique she had created for herself. It wasn't like she was the only artist who used blood or other bodily fluids in her work. Clearly, though, she didn't want it known. She wasn't making a point or statement with it. Not a public one, anyway. That was intriguing.

"Do you always paint with blood?" I asked.

"Yes. Yes, it's my 'thing.'"

"Always yours?"

"...Yes."

"Isn't it a bit of a lonely thing if no one knows?"

"A little. And, well, a few people know. People I trust."

We were spooking her, but she couldn't, or wouldn't run. We had a secret of hers, and she didn't trust us.

"Neave," I said, "We don't want to make you uncomfortable, or afraid. And I might know a way to put you more ease."

"Oh?"

"Yes." I looked over at Daci and arched an eyebrow. She shrugged, leaving the decision to me. "I'll trade you our secret for yours."

I smiled full at Neave.

She seemed uncertain, not reassured by a stranger's smile, but then she noticed my mouth, my teeth.

"Oh!"

And there, then, something happened. I felt the adrenaline rush through *her*. The flight reflex grabbed at her, but quick on its heels came something else, a hot rush of arousal. It fairly radiated from her.

It caught all three of us by surprise, and gave Daci and me a bit of pause.

Over the last century, the evolution of vampire "culture", or rather the perception of what vampires are and mean in modern culture, has been amusing to watch. People have much almost right, and so much so wrong.

There are times it works to our advantage. There are enough fetishists in the world, especially in the big cities, who will happily play with us. Some of the gothic romantics love the role of seduced victim, and remain blissfully unaware—or at most mildly suspicious—that the games are in fact quite real. Some even pretend to "turn", something they should be grateful they know nothing about. We make sure to disabuse them of the illusion and keep their lines between fantasy and reality as solid as we can, while taking what we need.

There are indeed few people who *truly* know, or recognize us for what we are: our own circle of trust and necessity in a shrinking world. For a moment, I truly worried that Neave was a closet fetishist, and her art a manifestation of a fantasy she knew nothing about. The fact I cared whether or not that was the case was something I hadn't felt in a while.

"You...you're real?"

Of course she knew the popular versions.

"Yes," I said. "But we're not like the stories or movies."

Her eyes were still wide, but there was something else — her own suspicion.

"I can't shape shift, or hypnotize you with my eyes."

"Or you would have done it by now. Yes, I know the game."

Her voice had a bite of anger now. She had seen pretenders.

"This is not a game, Neave," Daci said.

Neave's height was about halfway between Daci's and mine and, as she looked between the two of us, my eyes were drawn to her neck and the tension there. I could see the pulse, practically hear it—

"Prove it."

Now it was Daci's and my turn to glance at each other. We've been together a long time, Daci and I. A look says a lot.

I reached for Neave, bringing a hand around her shoulder and pulling her closer. I bent my head toward her, lifting her chin with my other hand until our lips met. The well behind her red lips called to me, and I let it. Her body, so stiff at first touch, relaxed and melted against mine. My tongue slipped past her lips into her mouth, and hers into mine, with a little moan.

Neave's tongue found one of my fangs, and explored it, sending a shiver through me. She probed it, testing to see if it was real, I imagine. Almost certainly by accident, she pricked herself with it. We both jumped—her from the tiny sharp pain, me from her taste. I cannot describe what that single drop was like. I sucked it from her retreating tongue, drawing its sweetness into me, and felt an old, long-tame beast rouse itself inside.

Daci's hand on my shoulder brought me back to focus. I was holding Neave tight to me, almost too tight. She breathed hard, pushing her body toward me, but pulled her head away. I let her break our kiss and stared into her wide eyes. Wonder was there, and the most delicious and strange combination of relief, fear, and yes—

"I want to see more of your work," I said. My voice was lower, colored by familiar wants. Not hypnotic, no, but I knew its power.

"My work?"

"Yes, take us to your studio."

My senses, all fully awake, opened to Neave, the sound of her heartbeat and the blood rushing through her veins, the red scent and lingering taste of her. Her *want*. All of it.

"Us?"

Daci leaned in close, her other hand on Neave's back. The three of us made a tiny inward-turned world, already receding from the people surrounding us.

"Us," she said, her tongue darting out to lick Neave's ear. The artist's shudder rippled against me.

It was blessed full dark as the three of us walked down the street. Neon and sodium lights painted the wet pavement and I at last took off my dark glasses. Neave's building was a few short blocks away, on a street that wore its past lives proudly. We walked there quickly, quietly, my arm around Neave's shoulder, Daci's around her waist. Neave seemed a little dazed.

"I've always wondered, since I was little," she said.

"But you were never sure," Daci answered

"They always seemed wrong. Too theatrical, too... Freudian."

At that, I laughed. "I'm sure he would have agreed."

Neave turned to me, questioning. I raised an eyebrow at her as Daci snorted, "He tasted of cocaine and cigars."

Neave shivered between us as we rounded the corner. Then she led us up five floors in a classic gated freight elevator activated by her key.

Neave's loft was mostly studio, with a small kitchen installed in one corner and a nest-like sleeping area in another – a futon piled with sheets and pillows. The kitchen and bed were clean, white contrasts to the rest of the unfinished space. Canvases, large and small, lined and leaned against the walls as well as gracing at least four easels in various positions on the floor. Paints, brushes, rags, all the various accoutrements lay everywhere, haphazard, but also well cared for. A palette of grays and reds was clearly the dominant color scheme in her work, but not the only one. The moon, a fat waxing crescent, shone through the abundant skylights and showed splashes of other color on her portraits, landscapes, abstracts. But each one harbored the scent of her. In each work, at least one color bore the tint of her blood. She pervaded the entire place. Daci and I both felt it.

As we stepped in, some of the tension left Neave's body. It felt very much like we were being permitted into a private place. Normally, this would be her place of power, I thought. But I think we had her more off balance than she was used to.

"Can I offer you something?" Neave asked. Her host's instinct obviously warred with others.

"Yes," I said.

"Oh? Coffee? Wine? Um—"

"No, none of that."

My arm was still around her shoulder. I turned her to face me and ran my free hand up her side. Daci stepped behind her and wound the fingers of one hand into Neave's hair, the other stroking down her belly to her thigh. She pulled Neave's head back, both to whisper in her ear and expose her neck to me.

"What would you offer us?" Daci asked. Neave shook all over. She met my eyes, terrified, wanting, all pretense of her as the huntress seeped away.

"Everything," she whispered.

Something older and haunted lived in her now. Something I certainly hadn't expected. But, oh, how it called to me. I lowered my mouth to her neck, my own pretenses teetering as Neave closed her eyes. I kissed her, wanting nothing more than to drink until I had devoured the whole of what she was.

"I *want* everything, Neave, but I won't take it. Not like that." The simple statement of self-denial made me boil. "We can't consume something as sweet as you all at once. It would be so selfish. Short sighted."

I was telling this to myself as well as Neave. My hand swept down her side, under the hem of her skirt, drawing back up against her skin and bunching the material above her hip. Daci did the same thing on her other side and, as my lips left Neave's neck, we slipped the one-piece dress over her head. Neave unconsciously moved her arms to help us slide the garment from her.

"But we accept your offer."

Daci and I pressed Neave between us, our hands roaming her body and each other's. Neave moaned out loud, sensuously; it was a sound of surrender I'd heard many times, but none quite so delicious as hers.

We covered the distance between the entryway and the bed without noticing, shedding clothes as we went, never for a moment leaving Neave completely free of our hands or mouths. The white sheets were perfectly clean, but piled and unmade, as if Neave had just gotten up from them. We fell amongst them in a tangle of limbs and hunger, for Neave had come alive. Her hands reached for me, for Daci. Her lips met mine, then my partner's. Between the wordless sounds of basic pleasure, with Daci and I sharing her breasts, my hand stealing down to the wet heat between her legs, Neave whispered once, and again...

"Yes."

Everywhere on Neave's body tasted different. Her lips still had lingering wine, her ear, the barest hint of jasmine perfume. A permanent air of paint and thinner adorned her fingers, and there my tongue found the exact spots she'd pricked to get the blood she mixed into her paints. That made me growl. Lower down, I tasted sweat, and soap, and Neave's own musk. Her pleasure, the chemistry of it, the psychic broadcast of it, those were as much what I needed, what Daci and I consumed, as anything else.

Neave bucked into my mouth as I pressed it between her legs. Her taste flooded me while Daci's kisses muffled the accompanying sounds. Minutes later, Daci and I had traded places and my mouth was back at Neave's, while her hand wrapped around my cock. Blindly, she pulled my hips between her open legs, where Daci was fervently busy. Daci's soft hair tickled my abdomen as she slid just to the side.

"Let me, dearest," Daci's voice came from below. She disengaged Neave's hand from my cock and took it in her own grasp. Daci's tongue swept between Neave's body and mine, as she lined me up to Neave's molten-hot slit. I took Neave's hand in mine, guiding it up Daci's body to the zenith between her legs, where Neave's fingers began their own exploration of sparse curls and pink folds.

Daci's head made way as I slowly sank into Neave. All of us groaned, even Daci, from the infectious aura of sex the three of us generated, as well as from Neave's fingers. The very air throbbed, as if our three heartbeats had become synchronous and magnified. The pulse and rush of blood was a liquid undercurrent to each beat. It was almost time.

One of my hands held Neave's, our fingers interlaced against the sheets above her head. With the other, I raised her chin. Turning her head, baring her neck to me. Neave shuddered and heaved under me, bucking toward my cock. I knew what Daci was doing as I felt her head turn against my thigh. Daci was pushing Neave's leg to the sheets, so she could reach Neave's femoral artery, Daci's favorite spot. She was also probably trapping Neave's other hand against her own slit, guiding our captive beauty to where she was most wanted, most needed.

"Oh, God!" Neave whispered. She sounded desperate, frightened, wanton. Thrusting deep into her felt so, so good. I raised my head, inhaling deep, fangs fully bared. Neave's wide eyes slid to my face, stared, then closed. Her entire body, taut and twisting under us, just seemed to melt. Oh, surrender, the sweetest taste of all.

I lowered mouth to Neave's neck and bit, flooding with her. Simultaneously I buried myself in her and came. At the edge of my awareness, I knew Daci's teeth also pierced Neave's flesh, just below the crease of her thigh, her well twice opened. Seizing, Daci emitted that low lusty sound I've loved for centuries. Neave's slack body spasmed as if shocked, rippling and clamping down on my jetting cock. And Neave, beautiful Neave, cried out, lost and exultant, keening as she gave herself over.

Words are useless to describe the essence one takes— and gives—at a time like this. Neave's blood tasted like blood, life itself to us, because we cannot create our own. Her pleasure— hormones, endorphins, psychic energy, all of that was the other half of what sustained us, and it tasted on the tongue and in the spirit, sweet and hot. Multiply all that by the pure physical pleasure of skin on skin, skin in skin, fluid heat, and it describes a shadow of what it truly feels like.

Moreover, it's an exchange of sorts. I didn't just come in Neave. Our fangs, our minds gave her some of what we were, too: tiny slivers of almost eight hundred years of pleasure, and a little pain, and so many other things. One could hear all of that in her cries, if one listened. And I did.

Lost in "now", our climactic pulse throbbed. Daci and I sucked and swallowed, our three bodies surged into each other, and Neave's shattered voice wailed. My mind burned in a yellow haze, like the full morning sun from my youth.

I could have remained there forever, in the sunlit field, feeling its warmth, but staying too long would be dangerous. Deadly. I was already pulling away from Neave's neck, leaving two scarlet beads behind, when Daci's hand found mine and squeezed: her gentle reminder. I was proud I had lost the need for it, yet still grateful for it. I always would be.

I raised my head and gaze down at Neave. I know I looked both drunk and feral at the same time. Daci's head came up as well. Her hand released mine and moved to Neave's cheek, wiping away the tear it found. Our Irish beauty was even paler, more magnetic than before. We'd not taken her into real danger, less than a pint each. She was strong and would recover quickly. Her rapid breath was already slowing, wild heart calming.

"Oh, my God," Neave struggled to speak, "A-Alak... D—"

"Shhh, sweet one," Daci said.

"Rest now," I said, smoothing a damp lock of hair from Neave's sweaty brow. "You have questions. I know. Later."

Neave nodded, already fading. Then her hands jerked, grabbing at my wrist and Daci's. Her eyes suddenly wide, scared, darting between our faces.

"Don't leave!" It was a whisper, but a plaintive entreaty, "Please... don't leave."

Neave burned the last reserves of her strength with this spark of worry. I didn't have to look at Daci, I knew what her face would tell me. "We won't. I promise."

Neave's sigh, of surrender to sleep, of abject relief, wormed its way under my skin.

Daci and I lay with her for a while, basking in her glow, watching her sleep, touching each other languidly.

"I didn't expect this out of our evening," she mused.

"Nor I. But life is interesting that way."

"That's why it's worth living, isn't it?"

"One of the reasons."

I leaned over Neave to kiss Daciana. Our artist's taste mixed with my savior's to create something new again.

Daci glanced up at the skylight-covered ceiling. "If those don't have shades we can close, we're going to have to wake her up before dawn," she said.

I smiled, leering. "We're going to wake her up before dawn regardless, love."

"Insatiable, Alak."

"Guilty, Daciana. Let me show you."

It was like a drug. Neave's blood sang in me, and I knew it did the same for Daci, When I lunged for her, rampant and ready, she rolled with my attack and pinned *me* under her. She smiled down at me, holding my arms above my head, trapping my cock between us. I out-massed Daci by, maybe, twenty-five kilos, but she would win if I fought her. I briefly considered it, just *to* lose to her, but I wanted her too much, and she saw that.

She lifted herself over me until I sprang up between us, then lowered, sinking her cunt down around my shaft. We moaned into each other, and she released my arms so I could crush her to me.

Later, as Neave slept, we explored the loft apartment enough to discover the antiquated blackout shades and draw them. They would do. Later still, maybe four a.m., we did wake up Neave. All of us still naked, we led the half-asleep woman to the center of her studio and took her there, half limp between us. I stood behind her, supporting and sliding into her as she ground back to me. Daci began at Neave's lips, kissing deeply before nipping a path down her front, until she could lick both Neave and me as I fucked the lovely painter. This time, we each took just the tiniest tastes—just a bit of real crimson to the blood tint of our lust, to call the pleasure crashing back down on her and us, until we all sank to the floor in a tangle of limbs and paint rags.

Eventually, I felt the sky color grey on the other side of the shades, and Daciana's morning nerves arrived. She curled against me, her protection from the dawn. Sunset has always been my bane, echoes of the past when it had meant something truly terrifying. For me the dawn always makes me feel I can push my luck just a little bit catch a glimpse of something real and unfiltered and long, long past. But histories differ, and Daciana's anathema is the rising of the star.

Also, this morning it wasn't just us huddled in the darkness. Neave was here. Neave, who had given herself to us as much as we'd taken her. And she was on her feet, if somewhat unsteady.

We watched in fascination as, almost in a trance, she grabbed a canvas and began covering it. The only light she used was a single small lamp. She used brushes, palette knives and her fingers, filling the portrait rectangle with three vague shapes in grey and black. The style of the quickly emerging piece was the same as that of the portrait at the show, and though she weaved and stumbled here and there, Neave worked steadily, bringing out three recognizable half-faces from the murky background. My nostrils flared as Neave touched clean fingers to her neck and her thigh, collecting thickened drops and smearing them into the pigments directly on the canvas. It was beautiful.

The sun was up now, on the other side of the black, and I could see where the coverings were imperfect, the glare of the sun, barely noticeable to Neave, but nearly blinding to me crept through a seam here and there. I was about to tell Neave what I had to do now, when she stepped back from her work with a critical, but half closed eye.

"Am I... *yours*, now Alak?

There were so many answers to that, depending on what she actually knew, what she guessed or assumed.

"In a way, Neave. It's not like the movies..."

"You said that before."

"Yes." I was tired now, too. "Daci and I need to get into the bed, under the covers for a while." A while— sunset.

"Oh... Of course. Do you need more blankets? More cover?"

"Yes, something opaque would be nice."

"You know, you belong to me now, too," she said, pointing to the painting. She'd crossed over to where I was standing myself up, cradling Daciana in my arms. Daci had taken refuge against the morning in sleep. She knew I would take care of her. Neave stumbled and sagged against me, almost bringing all three of us down.

"I think we all need to rest now."

"Yes."

I lay Daci in the bed and Neave crawled in after, pointing to a chest from which I retrieved a light wool blanket. I draped it and entered the bed on the other side of Daciana, so that her small form was nestled between Neave and me. Our artist was almost asleep already.

"See you in the evening," I said.

Neave smiled as I pulled the cover over Daci's head and mine, and reached her arm across us both. We fell into the new day's sleep.

* * * *

The Taste of B Negative
© Cheyenne Blue

I saw a shadow melding with the pooled darkness in the corners, where the dim nighttime lighting didn't reach—a dark more opaque and complete than the shifting patterns of gray. I knew enough to look away, to fix my gaze on the blip of the ECG, and on the patient's chart in my hand.

There are some things it's better not to acknowledge.

* * * *

I leave Constance in bed in the morning, the drapes pulled tight against the day. Her russet hair spreads over the pillow, her skin albescent in the dim light. There's a translucence about her today, and she seems to fade into the sheets, each soft exhalation pulling her down, spreading her thinly over the world.

I have to see my mother and buy my groceries—a gourmet selection of TV dinners for one. The car needs gas, and is overdue for its emissions test. I seldom go out in the mornings anymore, and these things get pushed aside. Instead, I spend my time on the bed, curled around Constance, listening to her breathe.

* * * *

"You're looking pale, Amelia," says my mother, her bony fingers caressing her morning martini. "Are you eating properly?"

The lettuce on her plate seems to wilt under my gaze. Lettuce, cherry tomatoes, celery sticks and low-fat Ranch—my mother's daily diet.

"Better than you." I take a bite of my rare-cooked burger for emphasis. It nearly chokes me, even as the hot coppery taste of scant-cooked beef makes me salivate.

Do cows have blood groups? O negative tastes stale; the universal donor has all the individuality sucked out of it. AB positive bursts with life and freshness. B negative is tangy, like gin and tonic with a slice of lime. It's her favorite.

These are the things that Constance tells me when the nights are long.

* * * *

Intensive Care is never still. It pulsates quietly with a muted throb. Life forces draining, some with a sigh, passing quietly, some with the cacophony of the cardiac arrest team. Crash call on ICU. They occur more frequently than average here, and questions are being asked. The hospital board taps its silver pen and wonders why.

I'm a qualified anesthetic nurse. It means I can intubate patients, passing the plastic tube down their trachea, inflating their lungs with a steady rhythm. The muscles on my hands between thumb and first finger bulge like golf balls from the repetition. And I'm the one who sets up the intravenous, a central venous line whether they need it or not. It never hurts to be safe. It's second nature for me to slide the cannula into the vein and cover the puncture marks with tape.

* * * *

Constance tells me tales of her childhood. She's old; it was long ago in the weave of time. In the telling, her eyes shift away from mine. I wonder if she's lying. The tiny inconsistencies niggle in my mind, and I open my mouth to clarify a point.

She sees, and covers my lips with a kiss. It's slow, and her tongue slides over mine, hot, wet, and wicked. She tastes of the night and all things dark. My question is lost in the curtained room.

She draws me down onto the bed and lets me worship her pale limbs. Her breasts are alabaster white. I trace their slight curves with my tongue. Her nipples are the reddest things about her, as sweet and hard and red as cherries. She likes me to bite them, hard enough that my teeth leave bruises on her skin, cloudy crushed purple marks on her white flesh.

"Harder," she says, and although I'm afraid I'll hurt her, I bite hard enough that my teeth meet the resistance of her flesh.

I've never drawn blood, no matter how hard I bite, how deep the gouges I leave on her back as she fucks me with her strap-on.

Once I asked her if I would become like her if I tasted her blood.

She laughed. "If you can find any."

I was afraid to hurt her after that. I'm not sure I love her that much.

She sighs and pushes my head down lower, to between her thighs, already parted to receive me. Her cunt doesn't taste like other women's. She tastes sharp and metallic, as dangerous as the barrel of a gun.

When she's weak and hungry, it takes longer. Her cunt shivers around my fingers and her juices are less. All of her life is slowing down. But I persist, and use my tongue and fingers in the steady rhythm she loves best. Her hands slide down and fist in my hair.

"Oh," she says, and I hear the wonder in her voice. It's as if each time is the first for her.

It's not the first, far from it. Her previous lovers span the centuries in a chain of love and lust. I wonder how it is for her each time they pass on and she remains.

Her fingers clench and release in my hair in counterpoint to the contractions of her cunt. When she's come, she pulls me up to her again. My head rests on her soft, white breast and I hear the steady thump of her heart.

"I love you, Amelia," she says, and her pale eyes are almost warm. "My sweet human girl. I love you so much."

And then it's my turn as she shows me how much she loves me, worships me, needs me.

"What do you want?" she asks, as her mouth tracks its way around my body. "What do you need?"

I need to be touched, to be caressed and stroked, to be fucked hard and long until every cell in my body is attuned to her.

The strap-on is in the drawer, but she's too weak to use it. Instead her fingers strum my clit, slip through my pussy lips, pushing inside me, in and out until I'm helpless with pleasure.

I like it when she goes down on me, when she parts me with her long fingers and presses her mouth to my sex, lapping me with her tongue until I'm slick and my juices coat my thighs.

Once, my period came when she was eating me out. She stilled, and her hand trembled on my belly. And then she pressed her face to my cunt and lapped and licked and sucked, pushing her fingers up inside me and then licking them clean. I came, and came again, and then, oh god, one more time. When she finished and moved up to kiss me, I saw the blood on her mouth and knew what had happened.

"It's all right, sweet girl," she crooned. "It doesn't happen like that. You're still my sweet human girl."

95

I saw her face through a cloud of tears. Constance kissed them away, and my blood was coppery on her breath.

Tonight, she just uses her fingers. They caress my clit, tremble on my lips. I come with a sigh and then we stay quiet for a long time, holding each other tightly in the dim room.

* * * *

"I'm hungry," she says later, much later, and her pale eyes take on the coldness of the ocean.

"You'll have to wait," I snap. "There are already questions about the number of cardiac arrests in my department."

She holds up a hand. It shakes with an elemental quiver. "No. I must feed."

"There are other hospitals in Baltimore."

"Well-lit hospitals, with vigilant staff and no dark corners."

"Are you saying—?"

She cuts me off with her lips on mine and her hand on my breast. My nipple blooms, and my protests are silenced. As she had known they would be.

* * * *

My mother calls before my shift. "He's left me again." The hardness in her voice reverberates down the line. "The bastard left with *her*."

Her. A Lolita, younger than me. My father's mistress, with her flippy skirt and flippy hair, skinny legs and girly giggle. I imagine my father between her thighs. Slender thighs, devoid of cellulite. I've thought about being between them myself.

"He'll be back," I say with a confidence I don't feel. Three times in as many months I've said those words to her. So far, each time I've been right.

"He will," my mother agrees. "I've canceled his credit cards."

* * * *

I wait out my shift in nervous anticipation. For Constance will come, and there will be the crash call, the lights, the controlled scurry, the jolt of defibrillator, and blood soaking into the bed from the intravenous site that will not stop bleeding.

There are three patients in ICU. I patrol the unit, sending the aide for an extended meal break. "It's quiet," I tell her. "I can manage."

This morning's surgery patient is sleeping quietly. I check his dressing, take his readings, turn the monitor so that the thin green line can't be seen as easily from the nurses' station. He's only in ICU as he has a wallet to match his stature. He's a minor Vanderbilt and they pay their bills. No other reason for him to be here.

The road traffic accident is waiting for organ harvesting. They pronounced her brain-dead this morning, but there's maneuvering to get the next of kin to sign the consent to remove her kidneys, her liver, her corneas, maybe her heart and lungs. She would be my choice. She's A positive.

The maternity patient brought in from the labor ward this morning is perilous. Her ECG leaps and skitters in uneven rhythm. But she'll make it, Constance willing.

She doesn't come that night.

* * * *

"He needs the young ones; it's a man's nature to hunt. It makes him feel important. I'm too old for him and he doesn't find me attractive any more."

My mother twists a napkin around and around in her fingers, dabs her mouth although she's yet to take a bite. A third martini sits and she drains it in one gulp, discards the olive.

I want to stab my absent father with the fish knife. Fillet him good, ease his flesh from his ribs to expose his pulsating ruby heart.

My mother's bony knees rattle together underneath the table. "He'll be back."

My lips twist. He's AB positive.

* * * *

Constance has the pallor of a snowdrift, and her oceanic eyes seek mine accusingly.

"I waited because you asked me. But I'm so hungry."

Love is the best distraction. I ease myself down on the bed beside her, gather her slender form to me, press my lips to her neck, over her jugular. Her hair is brittle and her skin papery. I asked her once if Vitamin C shots would improve its condition. She'd laughed. "If you can find a vein."

Her veins are deep rivers, buried like her bones. The shallow pulsating exuberance of blood is for others.

I kiss her, although her breath is fruity with ketones. I love her so much.

* * * *

"He sent me a letter." My mother's fingers shake and the paper flutters to the table to balance precariously on her garden salad.

I watch it hover then fall, one corner in her untouched Ranch dressing. "What does it say?"

"She's pregnant with his child. He's not coming back. They're moving to Denver to start a new life." Her laughter is empty like her martini glass. "Denver!"

He'll be in the shadow of mountains bigger than he is. I place my hand over my mother's and try not to flinch at the feel of her bones moving together.

* * * *

Constance's eyes plead with me. It's my shift again tonight. The barest of nods gives permission. What else can I do?

* * * *

The same three patients. The fat Vanderbilt shouldn't be here; he's upset the aide, and is shouting that he should have unlimited visitors. I tell him there's no place for him in this unit if that's the case, and he subsides. His face is yellow in the glow from the ECG. I flip his chart and check his blood group. O negative. Stale and sulfurous like the man himself.

The aide is in tears and won't enter his room. When the clock moves to the early morning hours, I pretend sympathy and send her for coffee. The early morning hours are the coldest, the times when the body's rhythms are weakest. When patients die—or are taken.

The telephone shrills. It's the Operating Room telling me to prepare for a new patient. A trauma victim, a car wreck on the interstate. A female, age 23, crushed sternum, internal injuries. Even as I'm summoning the aide, powering up the monitors, taking the cover from the ventilator, I'm wondering what shadows will be left in this night for Constance.

The patient arrives and I recognize her instantly, even under the blue operating room cap, even with her face mashed and distorted by surgical tape and partially obscured by the endotracheal tube's fittings. I hope she lost the baby—my half-sibling. I hope the fetus was pulped through a suction bottle and emptied down the Operating Room's drains.

* * * *

I see a shadow, melding with the pooled darkness in the corners, where the dim nighttime lighting doesn't reach. I see a dark more opaque and complete than the shifting patterns of gray. I know enough to look away, to fix my gaze on the blip of the ECG, and on the new patient's chart in my hand.

She's B negative.

* * * *

You'll Love the City
© Naomi Bellina

New York is the place to be, they said. You'll love the city. So he left his home of many years and came to New York. Found an old house off the beaten path with a basement for the daytime and a skylight to watch the stars at night.

So far, Dekel hated the city. It was too loud, too bright at night, and smelled like a sewer. Way too many people, which was usually a good thing for him, but not here. Not when they were everywhere, all the time, making noise, throwing their garbage in the street, pumping their waste into the water and the air. No, New York was not the place to be, not for him.

Tonight he left the sanctuary of his house and headed for din of the city. Shielding his eyes from the glare, he stepped out of the cab into the bright lights of downtown. Chaos. Utter chaos. So much noise.

It was a great spot for hunting, though. He had to give it that. Sit in a club, sniff out his prey. With his good looks and expensive clothing, the ladies flocked to him like moths to a flame. All he had to do was turn on a little charm and they were ready to climb their hot little asses into a taxi and come back to his lair.

Though he could easily have killed and disposed of his victims in this town, with no one the wiser, he'd learned long ago how to sip gently, like a connoisseur of fine wine. When he took care with his prey, he could have the same vintage over and over, if he desired, then move on to something else when he was bored.

That was the problem these days. They were all starting to taste the same. He'd had such high hopes for this century, dreams of exquisite samplings of sweet, succulent tastes. Things were not working out the way he envisioned.

Damn, this music is atrocious! Steeling himself for the half-hour or so he would have to spend in this den of bedlam, he settled in at the bar and ordered a drink. Alcohol used to give him the tiniest buzz, but no more. Nothing gave him much pleasure anymore. He drank only to stay alive, such as it were, hoping to find something, anything, that would spark his appetite and stir his soul again.

For Dekel, eternal life wasn't all it was cracked up to be. After the first hundred years, he was bored. A quiet, decent person in his human life, he couldn't stomach the atrocities his fellow vampires enjoyed, which seemed to keep them entertained century after century. Once he'd accumulated a few million dollars, traveled around the world, seduced and screwed a myriad of desirable women, he was tired. Yes, he could have ended it all, stepped into the fiery hot rays of the sun, but some deeply rooted self-preservation instinct wouldn't allow that. Still optimistic, he hoped to find something to spark his passion. Any day now.

Be one of the first to experience the magic of cryonics, they'd said, and at the time, it had appeared to be exactly the cure for what ailed him. He could sleep away a couple of dull centuries and would wake up in another time, years in the future. Surely the twenty-first century would hold something to interest him. One of his fellow vamps, a genius far ahead of his time, had started a secret cryonic lab, which he swore would work beautifully. Dekel would be put to sleep, then automatically awakened at a predetermined time. All very controlled.

So here he was, in 2012 less than a year awake, and bored already.

Looking around the room, he spied a tasty morsel. When she turned his way, something about her scent, wafting in his direction, intrigued him. He stared across the room at her until she sauntered over, and slid a pert little ass cheek onto the stool next to his. After the initial tedious pleasantries and drink buying were done, Dekel went to work.

"You are getting sleepy," he said, staring into her eyes.

"Huh? No I'm not. What the hell are you doing, trying to hypnotize me?" The juicy morsel, whose name had already escaped him, leaned away from him.

"You're not getting sleepy?"

"Hell no I'm not, and I better not be, with what I paid for that coke."

"You drank a cola and that is keeping you awake?"

"No, you weirdo. I snorted cocaine. That's keeping me awake. Listen, thanks for the drink but I think it's time for me to go." She slid off the stool, pulling her short skirt down.

Cocaine. Whatever that was, he wanted to know more. This woman smelled even better up close, like fire and heat. Her dilated pupils told him something riotous was going on in her body.

"I would like to try some of this cocaine. Can you buy it for me? I have a lot of money." Dekel pulled out a wad of cash as thick as a sub sandwich. Though the gesture was crude, he found it quite effective for getting people, especially women, to do what he wanted. This one was no exception. Her eyes opened even wider and she licked her lips.

"Shoot yeah, I can buy us, uh, buy you some. Come on, there's a place right around the corner where a dude hangs out, usually has something." She took his arm and led him to the door."Tell me your name again, sugar?"

"My name is Dekel. If you would be so kind as to repeat yours..."

"Lela. Remember that, you could be screaming it later."

"What?"

"Never mind, it's just a little funny saying."

"Oh, I understand. A sexually provocative statement. Yes, I hope there will be screaming later."

They smiled at each other, Dekel's grin not as wide as Lela's. He felt his fangs descending with excitement and didn't wish to scare her away.

True to her word, Lela found cocaine and they headed back to Dekel's house. He was becoming more aroused by the minute, thinking of this new sensation he was about to experience. Lela talked non-stop, and twitched and squirmed incessantly. If the drug produced this effect on her, surely it would do something for him.

She prepared the white powder, and he followed her lead, snorting a line up his nose. Nothing.

"Give it a minute or two. Sometimes it takes a bit to start working." Lela was already bouncing around, checking out his collection of books and erotic paintings on the floor-to-ceiling shelves and paneled walls. "You got some neat stuff her, Dekel. You collect pictures of naked people?"

"Yes, I collect antique erotica. I'm not feeling anything. Should I inhale it again?"

"Try a little more, but don't do too much. You don't want to overdose on your first try, right?"

Dekel tried one more toot, then sank back in his chair, disappointed again. Yet another thing in this century that didn't work for him. Well, the evening shouldn't be a total loss. Smiling at Lela, he held out his hand.

"Come here, I want to show you more of my artwork."

Lela followed him into his bedroom, and ooed and ahhed over the paintings. Dekel stood close behind her, brushed the hair away from her neck, and licked her soft skin. With a quick nip of a fang, he drew blood.

Lela yelped and grabbed her neck. "Ow! What are you doing? Did you just bite me?"

"I'm sorry, my dear, I only wanted to kiss you. I must have got carried away." Dekel took a step back and blinked. What was this sensation rushing through his body? A tingle of intense pleasure, a burst of white-hot energy tickled his spine. It must be the cocaine. He wanted more—more!

Summoning all his power, he gazed into Lela's eyes.

"Come, lay down here with me. It will be fine if I bite you. It won't hurt."

"Well, okay, but not on the neck. I'm a model, I can't have marks on me."

"Then I'll taste a hidden spot."

Dekel eased down onto the bed with her, pushed her skirt up and spread her legs. There, that luscious crease where thigh met pussy! He licked her musky sweat, then gently sank one fang into her tender skin. Lapping up the thin rivulet of blood that trickled out, he thought he'd died again and gone to heaven. Jolts of electricity coursed through his body. He hadn't felt sensations like this when he was human, let alone as an undead creature. Another nick and more of her precious blood flowed into him.

"Say, as long as you're down there..."

During his many years of sexual encounters, Dekel had learned how to please women. Their juices after orgasm held a bit of power, and with the tiniest bit of suggestion, they allowed him access to this luscious fluid. Ripping off her panties, he spread Lela's legs further apart and positioned himself between them. His tongue found her clit, already hardening, and he licked it lightly. A deep moan from Lela let him know he was on track.

Rubbing it ever so gently with one finger, he slid two from his other hand into her opening.

"Damn, you got some cold fingers, Dekel, but that's okay, it feels good."

"What else feels good for you, Lela?"

"Well, I kind of like my ass fingered too. Here, I've got some lube in my purse."

Taking the tube she handed him, Dekel inserted one more finger into her tight anus, eliciting another moan. She squirmed and wriggled in his hands, while he alternated lapping at her clit and the cut he'd made. More and more energy filled his body, and to his surprise, he felt something happening that hadn't occurred for a long time. He had an erection!

Pulling his fingers out of Lela, he undid his pants and dropped them to his ankles. There it was, a magnificent, rigid shaft, like steel. He touched it, squeezed it, and began to stroke himself.

"Hey, what about me?"

Dekel turned towards his companion on the bed. Normally, he pleasured women with his mouth and fingers, in exchange for drinking their blood and licking their juices. He hadn't put his cock inside a woman for quite a while, and gazing at Lela's slick, wet pussy, he decided it was time to do so.

"Take your clothes off," he demanded. Quickly he removed his own.

Not quite ready for the intimacy of face-to-face, Dekel pulled her to edge of the bed and up onto all fours, so her luscious ass was facing him. As he slid his cock into her, he felt a rush of ecstasy. This favorite part of his body, which had given him such pleasure while he was alive, was being stimulated once again.

"That is one cold cock, baby. Keep it moving, I'll warm it up." Lela moved rhythmically with him, pumping and squeezing his rod. She came with load moan, arching her back, and though nothing shot from his cock, he felt a frisson of pleasure that resembled the orgasms he used to experience.

"That was a lot of fun, Dekel," she said as they lay together, his leg crossed over hers, but otherwise not touching. "I've got an audition tomorrow. You want to come with me? We'll get some lunch afterwards?"

"I sleep during the day. But I would like to see you again tomorrow night. Can we do more cocaine?"

Dekel could already feel the effects wearing off, which was just as well. It would be time for slumber soon.

"Sure. Give me some cash, I'll get more. "

For the next week, Dekel reveled in the new sensations of cocaine and enjoyed the old ones of sex. Having derived most of his small bits of pleasure from drinking blood for the last century, this new activity was delightful.

"Let's get some pot," Lela suggested one night.

"What is pot?"

"You know, marijuana?"

Dekel had looked up marijuana, as well as several other drugs, on the Internet. One of the first conveniences he'd decided to take advantage of in this century was a computer. He'd had one installed and set up by a tasty young college student, who liked to be spanked while he drank. She gave him lessons on how to use his new toy, and Dekel was soon quite proficient.

Ready to try something new, Dekel agreed, and soon they were sitting on a couch in someone's home, lighting up a joint. Dekel took a hit, after watching Lela to see how it was done. Nothing happened, not that he'd expected a reaction. He leaned in to kiss Lela, and let his fang graze the inside of her lip. As he licked the red drops, a lazy, mellow feeling came over him. Yes, that was more like it. A very different sensation than the one cocaine produced, but he enjoyed it all the same.

Their host put on a funny movie, and brought our snacks and beverages. Several more people arrived, and they all crowded into the small living room. Dekel and Lela moved to a bean bag chair, and cuddled up there. As they watched the television, she took his hand and put it under her skirt.

"I'm not wearing any panties," she said in a low voice. "Rub me a little, what do you say?"

"Right here? In front of all these people?"

"Sure, why not? They're all stoned. Even if they do notice, they'll just be jealous."

So Dekel fingered Lela's slick pussy while she squirmed in the bean bag chair. He pulled her shirt part-way off her shoulder, and cut and licked the skin on her breast.

"Hey you two," one of the other women said. "It's not nice to keep all that fun to yourself. Share."

"I don't mind sharing," Lela said. "Dekel, do you want to kiss Patricia?"

With Lela's blessing, Dekel sampled them all, like a buffet of blood, while they giggled and laughed and ate bags of Cheetos. He charmed the women to have slow, deep orgasms as he drank from their veins, and enchanted the men not to care. Everyone tasted a little different, and some of them he fondled and caressed as he sucked, enjoying the feel of their young bodies.

They continued this activity for two more weeks, alternating between pot and coke. Dekel was welcome everywhere, since he had a plentiful supply of drugs and money. One day, after a bit of Internet research, Dekel asked Lela to get some methamphetamine.

"Oh baby, I don't want to do crank. That stuff messes you up."

Dekel, however, did want to try it, and set about trying to persuade her. Lela knew his tricks, and wouldn't look in his eyes as he cajoled.

"You would look really good in that dress," he said, pointing to a women's magazine she was reading. "How about I buy that for you?"

Lela narrowed her eyes and considered. She was smart enough to know what the garment would cost her.

"I'll be needing some new shoes to go with that."

Soon, they sat at his kitchen table with a black mirror, a razor blade, and a straw.

"Now, we're only going to do one line. This is powerful stuff."

Lela took a snort, threw her head back, and whooped.

"That shit goes right to my brain." She pulled up her skirt and Dekel sunk his teeth into her tender thigh.

"Easy baby, this is good shit."

The moment her blood touched his tongue, light and color exploded in his head. Fire ran through his veins, and every cell in his body leapt to life. This was it! This was what he'd been searching for.

They stayed up all night, Dekel promising Lela more goodies for every line she did. They watched movies, talked, screwed, and as dawn rolled around, Lela pushed him away.

"You've got to get to the basement, darling. It's almost light."

Dekel had no desire to stop now. He doubted he would be able to sleep. He didn't want that death-like slumber. In fact, he was almost certain he didn't need to seek darkness.

He opened his front door and stepped outside, oblivious to Lela's frantic calls. The first glimmer of dawn came through the trees. He opened his arms wide and lifted his face to receive the warmth he'd missed for far too long. The meth had cured him. Why should he hide from the light? The sun was his friend.

He was, of course, wrong. The moment the first rays touched his skin, he burst into flame.

Lela watched in horror for a moment, then shut the door and set about wiping her fingerprints from every object in the house that she'd touched. She grabbed what cash she could find and a few items she thought she could sell. Leaving the meth on the table, she ran. She didn't look back at the pile of ashes smoldering on the pavement.

* * * *

It's Lovely. It's Horrible
© Kathleen Bradean

At some point, it stops being fun.

When you grab a delicious black-haired young thing in smudged eyeliner on the dance floor of a semi-legal basement club to devour his lips and grind against his hand so he can feel the drenched heat between your thighs, then you're all hair-pulling, lip-sucking want and need groping for the fire exit on your way to getting nasty against a bin in the alleyway and you find out he's a she, at least equipment-wise, but you don't give a shit because she knows instinctively to finger fuck you with three digits at once and bang her knuckles against your clit, it's wonderful.

At least it is the first ten or twenty or sixty times. But when you have to do it every night just to keep sane—when even the reeking drunkard who talks to himself on the metro platform backs away as you turn haunted, heavy-lidded eyes on him, appraising his cock while you absent-mindedly smear the rest of your red lipstick across the back of your hand, that's when you tell yourself how much you hate this damned game.

That's why I won't bite you no matter how much I want to sink my teeth into your nipple and feel the pop of your flesh ripping apart before the warm gush of blood. No, that isn't why. In honesty, I won't bite you because you're not It and I won't drag an innocent into this un-merry chase.

I'm not a vampire. See? Normal human teeth. I'm not one of those head cases who thinks she's a vampire either. It isn't about blood. It's about hunger. I have it and it's eating me up heart, soul, and brain. It's all I think about.

At the tag, the hunger spills into me. Suddenly, it's my turn to be the Seeker. Exhaustion can't hold me down.

And I am exhausted then, much as I am now. Tired of the pursuit; weary from catching the midnight train to Paris; the first flight to Dubai; jumping from the last rung of a fire escape in Manhattan; running, running, shouldering between the revelers thronging the streets of Stockholm after a World Cup win while my lungs sear, until It's cornered and I'm yanking up my skirt, lusting for the bite as much as I fear my coming turn.

This is when I lean forward, elbows on my thighs, chin resting on my hands, my smile working its magic on you. You know you should get up and move to another car in this train before we reach Cardiff because I'm talking crazy and there's a rip in the knee of my black stockings that reveals a scabby scrape.

Dodgy, you're thinking. The collar of my jacket looks as if it's the pelt of something that died from mange, even though it's as faux as the jet beads clattering between my small breasts—and yes, I saw your glance. They're the color of milk, you're probably thinking. If you look closely at them, you can see the blue lines of my veins under my skin and now your mind is wandering back to the vampire question but I assure you that I don't drink blood and I can walk in sunlight. I just don't have time to get a tan because all I have is this terrible, unquenchable hunger and the ravenous need to find It. All else pales, even my skin.

From the furrow in your brow, that admission has you worried. Ever since I plopped into this seat across from you, you've been casting glances at the other passengers to check what they might think of me, and of you. But you won't give up your seat because my eyes are wide and honest in that vulnerable doe way that brings out the chivalry in men. You're enchanted. You can't help yourself.

And aren't you just so presentable? That suit of yours is bespoke. I can spot the difference between very high end off-the-rack suits and custom tailoring. Your Italian shoes were shined this afternoon, after the rain. You're so exquisitely proper that you're simply begging to be mussed. A fine suit on a man—has no one ever told you this?—is like black lace French knickers and stiletto pumps on a woman. The stuff of dirty daydreams. I'll bet you've never guessed how many times your jacket has been mentally peeled from your shoulders, or how many women have imagined your long fingers gripping their hips from behind.

Oh now, I've spooked you. It isn't easy hearing that you've been reduced to a sex object. And yet, it's a bit flattering too, isn't it? I see that nervous smile. If you square your shoulders, lift your chin, and tighten that tie one more time, you're going to have trouble breathing, and I can hear how labored it is already. Acute hearing comes with the role of Seeker. I can also hear your pulse speeding up, and I know why.

Fear. Arousal. Your body can't tell the difference. Can your brain?

Nothing like this has ever happened to you before. Your life was preordained not to include a moment like this, only now I've come along and hopelessly befuddled all that, haven't I? Your life was supposed to be unremarkable, from birth to death. Right schools, right job, right wife... or is that husband? Don't bother to answer because frankly, my dear, I don't give a damn because before long you're not going to care either. It's part of the game, the way I can get to you, get past your preferences, make you share my hunger. You are so bored that even with every alarm clanging inside your staid mind you can't resist hearing me out because you're proud that I picked you from all the other people on this train and you so desperately want to be special, just once. Don't be insulted. Everyone feels that way. Everyone.

Our theory about the game is that it makes us exude pheromones, because we have no problem finding willing sex partners to temporarily quench our need. Ultimately, that delaying tactic stops working for us and we have to come together again. Have to. Want to. Desire is horrible and fantastic and frustrating and consuming. In the end, you need the Seeker so bad that even when you want to keep running you can't and the Seeker draws ever closer as you're trembling and standing on the edge of a precipice too afraid to leap even though you know the tag will bring relief. Fear. Arousal. The same thing in this game.

I'm going to get up soon. I'm going to walk down that aisle to the back of the car. You aren't going to turn to watch me even though you'll want to so badly that it will take every drop of your resolve to keep staring straight ahead. You're going to take your copy of the *Financial Times* out of that swell briefcase by your feet and snap it as if slightly irritated. And even though you've already read it, you aren't going to be able to remember a single word you're looking at. When you think that twenty minutes have passed, you're going to check your watch. You're going to see that it's only been seven minutes. Maybe eight. Whatever you do, you're not going to glance around to see if people are looking at you. You're going to open your paper to the second page and pretend to read it. If you check your watch again, you're going to be extremely discreet about it. Then you'll look at the scenery for a while. When twenty-two minutes have passed, you may come to the loo, or water closet, or whatever you call it where I will be waiting.

I said "may", because this is entirely up to you even though you might feel as if you've been compelled. You

114

have, but you haven't. "No" is a word I've come to worship. Sometimes I catch myself intoning it, "No, no, no," but by now it's a meaningless sound on my lips. It might still have power for you, though. I almost hope it does. And yet, while I'm still here, I'm cleverly attacking every weakness I can detect in you to get around your reservations because when you're starving, the temptation to steal a tasty morsel is almost unbearable. So please feel free to say yes.

Despite the fact that your cock is hard and you've already almost convinced yourself that it will be all right just this once to take what I'm offering to you, the moment I leave you're going to think about snakes and apples. You're going to question if a rational man would ever accept forbidden fruit especially when it appears as feral as I do. You're going to think of these things because I am putting the thought into your head. I want you, if only for a moment, to ponder the existence of God, of angels, demons.

When this first started, we called it a virus, but as the game continued, we began to speak of it as a demon. When you stop living in the real world and are driven by nothing but desire, you start to believe your existence might be hell. The need possesses us—transferred, we assume, by the bite, which is why no matter how overwhelming the urge, I won't sink my teeth into you. We've decided that this is a game for two, even if playing it kills us, because we can't bear the thought of dragging someone else into it despite how exhausted we are. I mentioned that before, didn't I? I'm so weary that I talk in circles. But I think even if my legs were broken, I'd still drag myself across the Gobi Desert by my fingernails to tag It.

The days immediately after the tag are anguish for both of us. We stay together even though we're like the same poles of magnets; we can actually feel the repulsion forcing us apart. But we endure it so we can spend some time together before the game begins again. We sleep, mostly. We squabble over who left the lavatory untidy. We sit in cafés, watch normal people from behind our sunglasses as if we're at the zoo, drink strong coffee and pick at our food. We spread salves over our bite wounds and apply bandages. It's all very domestic.

Anyway, I was speaking of the loo where I will be waiting for you. In the movies, sex against the wall looks hot, but I've learned to hate it. You're so much taller than I and it's hard to come when I'm standing. I'd offer to let you recline on the ground and straddle you, but really, I adore your suit. Honestly. I can't bear the thought of that material touching the piss splatters and damp squares of toilet paper on the floor of that bathroom, so I'll be the one rolling in the filth. Look at this outfit. Do you think it matters to me? Or, if you're feeling overwhelmed, I'll line the seat of the toilet with paper and you can sit like a king on his throne while I take your hard cock into me because I want to keep you tidy and clean just the way you are now. I want you to be able to go home to your proper life and look as if you hadn't had an adventure. I don't want any part of this to become real for you.

Ooh. I saw the sparkle in your eye. Adventure appeals to you. You were once the nation of privateers, bawdy Elizabethans and decadent Victorians. That blood still burns in your veins, does it? Lusty boy. I knew I picked the right man. If I didn't feel so protective of you, I'd slip my hand under my skirt and douse my fingers in my juices. I'd draw a wet line across your upper lip and dare you to taste it, although imagining your tongue makes me shiver. The thought of having you inside me has my clit puffed up and stiff. One flick, and I'd come. I'm as drenched and torpid as a tropical jungle. If I spread my thighs to release some of this heat that's driving me mad, my scent will fill this car.

I see your nose twitching. You're trying to smell me. Patience. I'll unbutton your shirt and draw runes across your chest in slick cunt juice if you want me to. I'll kneel on the fetid floor and unzip your trousers. My lips will slide down your shaft with a tight grip that will remind you of the only time you tried anal sex.

Do me a favor and don't come from just that. If only you knew how good a hard cock feels inside—or maybe you do. Tomorrow, when I wake, I want my pussy to ache. I want to know I've been fucked. I want a guilty smile to spread over my lips and a damp spot on my panties as I remember how nasty we were.

Do you want to know what women really want? They want to see all-consuming desire on their lover's face. Reason wiped out by pure lust for her. They want to see that they make you so crazy that you can barely control yourself. So don't be gentle. I hate gentle. Because you have such lovely fingers, so manicured, so long, I'll face away from you and hope you'll bruise my hips with them. I'd like that trophy. Ten perfect purple-yellow fingerprints on my skin. It would help me remember you.

Oh dear. That look on your face. Maybe we better wait thirty minutes instead of only twenty. You need time to cool down, but we don't have that long before we pull into the station, do we? Well, think of cricket, or England, or something dreadfully dull for the next twenty minutes then either come to me or don't. I hope you do. Sex is the only way to sate this hunger and I am so very, very hungry. Ravenous. It gets worse the longer the game goes on.

It's waiting for me in Cardiff. He just can't run any longer. I can feel him, every heartbeat, every fear, every longing. That's how the Seeker tracks It. This is part of our curse. It isn't love, this thing between us. Never was. We're trapped in mutual obsession. It's lovely. It's horrible. I wish it would end. I think it will kill me.

* * * *

The Curse
© M. Christian

Blood on the sheets. When she awoke: blood on the sheets. Not a lot, but enough. Even though she was alone, embarrassment warmed Ellie's cheeks as she stripped her bed and tucked them into the laundry hamper. At least they hadn't been new.

Alone? Slowly, memories surfaced past the beginning of her daily routine. Showering, washing herself, she remembered other hands... there, there, and there. The night before? As crimson spiraled away at her feet, down the drain, it seemed to be replaced by a quick storm of recall: the thumpa, thumpa, thumpa of the band on a distant stage, the biting sting of clove cigarettes and ganja in the air, the distant frostbite of a very cold beer in her hand. It was the perfect place, a lovely excuse – women everywhere, dancing under a painfully blue sky and then under hard industrial lights. Pride Day—a time to step out, wear the colors, be free. A special women's space, on a special gay day. But... Ellie had felt uncomfortable. For a while she'd watched, marching the route with the rest, becoming a part of the crowd. But then the isolation returned and she was just one among thousands. Just a face in that overwhelming crowd.

She recalled the depression, like a heavy blanket around her shoulders. So many women dancing around the outdoor stage, a parade of their own: all the pretty young girls moving with each other. Smiles, laughter. And all she'd wanted, desperately wanted, was someone to be with.

Company... Then someone had, someone had stepped in. A quick cascade, an explosion of fire-hued hair, huge dark eyes, lips that seemed to slyly smile from the poster of some silent-film queen, a lithe form—slender and graceful under the pulsing lights, the harsh street lamps, the tiny bulb of her car's feeble dome light, the harsh fluorescents of her lobby, the glow from her familiar lamps, then—lastly—the contours of her illuminated by the ember-red numbers of her night stand clock.

Twisting off the shower she stepped, wet and dripping into the bedroom, hoping for her—hoping to see her elegant eyes, brilliant lips, deep-throated laughter. But only covers on the floor, only a bare mattress waiting for her. Alone? Yes.

* * * *

She was almost late coming into work. Unheard of, though no one would have noticed. She'd stood and stared at the bare bed, looking for some kind of evidence, some kind of physicality to match her filling memory. They'd stood on the balcony, looking at the stars and the brilliant lights of the city. A natural position, Ellie's hands on the cold metal of the balcony, the other woman's hands around her waist, her breath on the nape of her neck. A cascade, Ellie remembered, of goose bumps, but not from the cooling night.

Hard daylight. Blinking, wrapped in a towel, she stepped out, looking for footprints, hand prints. Moisture, a sparkling flicker of dew, anything to prove it had really happened.

They'd kissed—yes, and she tasted her again in memory: the pressure of lips, the heat of her, the rhythm of their breathing. They'd come inside, kissed by the foot of the bed. The whisper of her black satin dress, the sudden too-tightness of Ellie's jeans. The surprising laughter when the kiss broke, when the high of their excitement crested. The way, then, the giggles had faded as she had put her hands on Ellie's face, traced the contours of her cheeks, her jaw, the way she'd tapped Ellie's nose, whispering "button" in a rich, throaty voice.

In the warming room, Ellie stood at the foot of the bed, turning so she was facing the way she remembered standing. Yes. Eyes brown with flickers of amber. Lips too full, too red, too silken to be anything but a fantasy running around in the real world. Lithe, boyish. She remembered how she liked to watch her move, liked to watch her walk barefoot across the apartment. Graceful, as if every muscle were elegantly conducted to some lovely score.

Her shoes? Yes... She'd kicked them off, near the foot of the bed. Without really thinking of the woman walking the hard pavement on thin, bare feet, Ellie dropped down to look, hoping for the reality of a simple black pump. Nothing, of course. Memories, but nothing else.

A glance at the clock brought up more—her face, glowing as if from low embers, smiling up at her. There, in her eyes was the lust Ellie'd wanted, needed, but also something else, something finer, softer, kinder. There was something else there, in the dull red glow, something that had made Ellie's heart melt as fast as her body. Liquid— yes, molten... .

A glance at the clock also brought a slap of reality. 8:05. Half an hour on the bridge, fifteen minutes from the garage to the office. She was going to be late.

Still, hurrying, there was no escaping the growing number of ghosts from the past, that expired night: brushing her hair brought up a voice, rich and rumbling, and the feel of strong fingers stroking the top of her head; doing her teeth was those same fingers brushing her lips, feeling them before another kiss...

Finally, she had to stop, had to put both hands on the edge of the sink and breathe deep. In and out. Strong, steady breaths. She was late, she needed to get dressed and get going. She had work to do, lots of work to do. If it had happened... if it had happened then it was nice, and that was all. It didn't change anything. If it hadn't, then the world was as it was. Ellie, her little place, her little life, her job—the days falling down, one by one.

Tears, hot on her cheeks. How she wanted it to be real.

Eyes open, puffy and red. Her face in the mirror, looking broken and small. But then she saw it, as real as a shoe, as foot and hand prints in night dew. Evidence, reality. Purple and harsh, sore, yes, but evidence none the less. A scarf would hide it, but not for now. Lateness, the bridge traffic, the walk from the garage, the firm, everything was gone from her mind. For now, as she stood in the window, the bruise on the slope of her neck was too priceless to hide, too real not to be stared at.

* * * *

The office normally seemed to exist out of time. Usually one day there melded into the next and then the next, as an endless caterpillar of files, meetings, filings, a slow dance of meaningless movements that seemed to have no function aside from filling days.

She'd smelled of lemons, strong and sharp. A bite to the nose, a sting as they'd kissed. Ellie was opening her first file of the day when the memory came, strong and fast. In an instant, she felt her body respond. Though shame bloomed on her face, she relished the new information, a few more details to the mystery.

She usually made small talk with the others— television of the night before, the day's headlines, something safe. But that day she walked through the office like a woman still asleep, lost in her vivid recall. *Lemons*, she thought accepting another load of papers, and hair... hair the color of rusted wire, a brilliant halo of light.

"Sure, no problem," she said to someone who stuck his head into her office, his face a mask of seriousness. She had no idea what she agreed to, her lips forming the dismissive words just to get him gone, to get him to leave them alone—just Ellie and her slowly dawning memories of the day before.

Jennifer, the little bob-haired girl from Shipping, stopped by when the clock was inching towards five, wanting gossip, both to pick up as well as give. "What did you do after the parade, hum?" she said, implying, suggesting, mocking because she suspected the answer was nothing.

Ellie wanted her gone as well. How do you put the bite of lemons, hair the color of a sunset, into dyke drama? Even bringing the woman up with Jennifer would be a kind of sacrilege, a Polaroid of Jesus on the cross. Instead, she smiled her best fake smile and said, "Not much."

The night didn't share anything else. The bed was just a bed, still no shoes shoved under, still no palm-prints on the railing. Only the mark on her neck, the fading reddish bruise, was all that remained—and even that seemed to be healing, fading into just plain skin.

* * * *

Her voice. The sound of it, the ringing timbre of her speaking, washed over Ellie as she opened the Peterson file. So strong, so realized in her ears, Ellie had to close her eyes to focus on its clarity. A lilting voice, full of honey and wine, with a touch of somewhere South, but not corn-pone. More white-painted mansions and the kindness of strangers.

"You from around here?" Ellie had said, regretting the stupidity of the line the instant the words had stumbled out of her mouth.

"Sometimes..." she'd answered, conjuring bayou and Savannah, with a brilliant smile. "Want to dance?"

So they had, a clumsy mating dance of the female of the species, full of suspicion and raw passion. They hadn't talked much during it, their voices crushed or carried away by the thumping bass of the Glamour Pussies from the stage. But then they did have a conversation, carried through the language of shaded eyes and pursed lips. No words, but intent nonetheless.

Before they feel asleep together, arms wrapped in a Gordian knot of spent passion, she'd said, words laced with Spanish moss and green drinks on the verandah, "I think I'll like it here."

* * * *

A day, maybe two. The Peterson file was open but bare of any work. Every hour it seemed, something new surfaced, some detail of that night. The glow of her skin, pale—almost translucent—but lit from within by some kind of raw light, pure energy. The ferocity of her love-making, as if she'd been trying to crawl inside Ellie. The throbbing of the bruise on her neck, the way her belle had smiled and licked at the chafe gently, apologetically.

"So, who is she?" Jennifer said, poking her bob-haired head around the corner.

Ellie blushed, warmth spreading down her neck. "Just someone I met."

"Oh! Just someone or a special someone?" Her eyes danced with excitement at seeing this side of Ellie.

"Special, I think," Ellie said. "I hope."

"You haven't heard from her?" Concern this time, maybe that sweet, innocent Ellie had been waylaid by the dyke version of a "wham-bam-thank-you m'am"

The thought had never occurred to Ellie. Hadn't heard from her? Had it really been days? No calls. No flowers. No letters. No U-Haul (to play to the old joke). Nothing. Yet there wasn't fear in that, wasn't that normal stomach-dropping shame of actually hoping for something good to happen. None of that. Just the soft, warm glow in her belly—the desire, the affection, remaining—undiluted, still there.

"Not really," Ellie said, her voice sounding lost, as if from far away.

"Oh, Ellie!" Jennifer said, moving around the corner to put a warm hand on Ellie's. "Don't take it too hard."

"I won't, I promise," she said, with mock sincerity, just to make the other woman go away. She wanted to be alone with the thoughts she was having, the warm swell of emotions. No, she hadn't heard from her. No, she didn't know where she was. But then it also seemed, somehow, like she'd never left.

* * * *

Getting up the next morning, a name: Samantha. The revelation was a bolt, a brilliant stroke through her, making Ellie's body respond. A smile. Samantha. Yes, perfect—a bell-ringing tone of truth. Her name was Samantha. Brushing her teeth, she remembered the color of her eyes: gray, like burnished steel.

Pulling on her pantyhose, she remembered her breath— sweet, a lingering touch of the beers they'd shared. She remembered the way it was hot on her neck after their first, consuming kiss. A slow pant that warmed Ellie's already burning skin. Sweet...

125

Driving to work, she knew that Samantha of the sweet breath had been slightly shorter, not enough to crane the neck, but enough to put the hesitant Ellie at ease.

Arriving—chocolate. Little Samantha with the sweet breath had asked if she'd had some. Ellie, whose face exploded if she had even a cup of coffee, had to disappoint. But Samantha, sweet Samantha, had just smiled and said that she'd get her own later. Then the kiss.

An hour later, Peterson file opened and ignored, she remembered her feet as they slept together, the way she'd kicked, like a cat in a dream of chasing mice, her rough nails scratching Ellie's tender ankles, drawing her out of her dream.

More, too much more. Panting with the cascade, Ellie locked herself in the bathroom for an hour, letting her body recall what her mind couldn't comprehend. She knew she was risking embarrassment, but didn't care— what was coming... . came.

Only Jennifer seemed to notice. She stopped by as Ellie was packing to leave. Concern darkened her face. "I just don't want you to get hurt," she'd said, then repeated the offer that Ellie should call if she needed to.

Ellie agreed, again just to get away, to get back to her memory of that one night. "Ah, will," she said, hearing the honey and Savannah tones slip out from between her lips: "Ah will, sweetie. Ah, will."

* * * *

Key in the lock: blues were her favorite music. Bathroom, water splashed on her face: she loved dark nights, no moon. Sunlight was alien, distant. Shoes off, dress thrown onto the floor: walking the streets of New Orleans long before they could even be called streets.

Women in hoop skirts, carrying umbrellas, elegant Creoles with their sing-song voices. Boys running by, chasing a wayward, and terrified, chicken.

The rest of it came off, naked and under the covers—shivering as if from a cold, a fever: yellow fever, people dying all around her. Healthy, she'd taken to theatrical symptoms to ward off suspicion, having to be careful about who she chose, not wanting to inherit the illness.

Covers over her head, body quaking: World War II, starched clothing and chafing nylons. Many soldiers, in and out; many women, lurking around Charleston—lost and hungry. She, just hungry. Much confusion, and in that an easy way of living. She missed wars. Because she could only be with women, she still missed the chaos, the frantic sloppiness of unrest. Peace was meticulous, peace was pedantic. People in peace had nothing better than to miss people, look for them, try and track them down.

Too much, a torrent, a heavy rain of images. Many faces, many times, many eyes looking at her with amused relief, many shoes on many feet, many nights with many women. Those eyes—always the same reflection, always the same attitude, always the same. Ellie, while there was an Ellie, realized the sameness, saw it with a shocking knowledge: always the same attitude, because no matter whose eyes they all housed Samantha—and she was looking in a mirror.

I love you, Ellie thought as it became too much, as she drowned under the heavy sea of Samantha's many years—loving her, caring for her, till the end.

* * * *

Later that night, the moon bright and new, she awoke, the storm having passed. Clarity. Nothing but today, nothing but her body under the sheets. Stiff, muscles quavering from strain and tension, she got up, looking at herself in the full-length mirror. The bruise was fading, as it always did, the stigmata of waking, the sign of another month.

One more month before blood on the sheets again. Slowly, getting used to new muscles, new bones, new tendons, her senses, Samantha got dressed.

I love you, too, Ellie, Samantha thought, looking at her face one last time in the mirror, car keys flashing silver in her right hand, *at least as much as I love myself.*

Then she smiled and went out.

* * * *

Red Wet Kiss
© Beryl Falls

Madison remembered an afternoon with him. David had bound her, wrists and ankles, to the bed posts. Usually he found a more awkward position for her but this time he said, "You could be here for a while." Then, using various means he'd forced her to climax until she begged him to stop. "If I come once more I'll die." He stood, watching her leak tears, and made her come again.

* * * *

"I'm here for her." Madison stood between the old woman trembling on the ground and the three youths who were slowly but deliberately approaching. One of the boys snickered.

"Yeah? Well we're here for *you*." He lunged at Madison. As she fell backwards over the old vampire at her feet, a blur of teeth hurtled between her and her attacker. The newcomer towered over the youth as he crawled away in fear and pain. In the dark she couldn't see the face of her savior, but the silhouette was unmistakable. David.

He strode slowly towards the other two, one of whom shouted, "You think the three of us can't take you?" David smiled. Instantly his hand grabbed the teen by the hair, and he buried his fangs in the kid's neck. A wet scream burbled as the throat was torn away. Blood sprayed skyward. David let the body fall to the ground, watching as the others fled.

Madison cowered against the wall in disbelief. David, whom she had missed every day—this was why he had disappeared from her life? He moved closer, though she still couldn't see his face.

"I think your friend is beyond help." He gestured toward the other body crumpled at her feet. "Too bad—plenty of blood here tonight." She knew he was smiling, and that his grin was bright red. "You wouldn't even need to prick that soft white skin of yours." She smelled the rancid odor of the old woman's death, her own fear, and blood. "But I don't remember you ever minding a little penetration."

She blushed and closed her eyes. When she opened them again he was gone. She exhaled, wondering when she'd stopped breathing. Part of her was glad he had run away. Part of her wanted to run after him. It was hours before she could think that she might have easily died—both if not for him, and because of him.

* * * *

It had been five years since the plague came: the vampires. Most people insisted the blood drinkers were just ordinary humans who believed they were vampires. A few organizations, though, knew the truth and acted upon the threat. The one Madison had joined dedicated itself to helping the afflicted to manage their disease by getting blood from legitimate sources. Their success rate was minimal, especially in the city where there were too many opportunities to hunt. Populations of undesirables became feed lots for hungry vampires. Still Madison went out once a week with her vials and pamphlets and opened her vein to those in need.

There were other groups who took a more direct approach to the problem, with fire and steel. She suspected some of her fellow volunteers walked both paths.

When David had left her two years ago, she'd thought she would die. He had been her only source of pleasure, of happiness, of life. So she could understand the need to get life from one bright source.

Now he was back and she felt the world recede again, as it had when she served him. Conversations seemed to be underwater—muted, dimly lit, unreal. All she could think of was seeing him again, and what he might do to her.

* * * *

"Looking for me?" Madison turned to the dark voice behind her. "Or will just any blood drinker in need do?"

"I've been looking for you for two years, since before... ."

"Before I was stricken? Or are you here on the side of God, to help me grapple with my demons—to let me suckle at that syringe you carry? To show me there's a better way?" He backed her against the wall and gazed down at her. "Let me tell you something. When I drink, it isn't in cc's. It's in gallons."

Wasn't this the man she had loved and served? Hadn't he loved her too? His eyes were iron, his lips pulled back in a crooked smile that revealed one canine. She'd never seen teeth that large, not in a year of working with the plague victims. He fingered her hair. In the sunlight it would have sparked with russet highlights. In the dim light of the alley it turned to dried blood.

"Thank you—for saving me," she whispered.

He threw his head back and laughed. "Saving you? Did it ever occur to you that I wasn't saving you *from* them, but *for* me?" He let his right hand drop to cradle the side of her face, and then lower to caress her neck. "The only reason I didn't take you that night was that I'd just drained someone else dry."

131

She shivered, raising her hands to his chest, knowing there was no way to stop him.

"I haven't fed in three days," he whispered, lowering his mouth to her neck, "and you smell so sweet..." That last a guttural breath against her skin.

Suddenly she heard her partner John's voice at the entrance to the alley, "Madison, are you okay?" David pulled away from her and turned to John, his eyes flashing even in the darkness.

"I'm okay, John. I know him." John hesitated as she continued. "You go on. I'm done for the night. I'm fine." He didn't seem convinced but nevertheless he retreated, out of sight.

David pushed away from her. "You think you know me? You don't know anything!" He paced with the jerking straight-backed gait of someone on the verge of physical outburst.

"This is going to happen. This is going to happen. It's just not going to happen here." He looked around the alley, at its decay. He turned and started to stride away. "Come on," he ordered.

"And if I say no?"

He paused, cocking his head to the side. "You won't".

He was right. She trotted to keep up with him as he disappeared into the night. Anyone they passed shied away from him and gaped at her. A young vampire leaning in a doorway snickered. "What you gonna do when you catch him?"

It was more a question of what he was going to do.

He stopped suddenly. "We need to lose the boyfriend now."

"What?"

"Your friend is following us. You want to lose him, or do I kill him?"

"No! I mean," she said, turning to look behind her, "I don't even see him."

"I wasn't really offering a choice," he said as he lunged and flung her across his shoulders in a rough fireman's carry. From then on their progress was swift. She felt ill from the jostling and blurred ground passing beneath her. It was a relief when he stopped to enter a darker space, paused, and then started up stair after stair.

The air was cool and smelled of dirt and damp stone. Finally he opened a door and carried her across the threshold. He dropped her just inside. She landed on her feet, but unsteady, afraid to move. He bolted the door behind them. Then there was silence, broken only by her breathing. She knew he could hear the blood pulsing in her veins.

"Sorry about the lighting. I don't need it, and I don't have visitors." He moved closer, behind her, his breath soft against her ear. "But this is hardly the first time I've asked you to do things for me in the dark."

She wanted to smile but did not. He was so angry, even under the banter. There was an edge to his voice she hadn't heard the whole time they were together. It frightened her.

It smelled like him in here, the old him. But how could that be? Vampires didn't sweat. They all smelled the same, like the air after incense had burned— something sweet, gone sharp and bitter.

He took her shoulders and backed her into the gloom, stopping at the place where he slept. His hand lingered on her shoulders, his thumb rubbing her flesh. He pushed the straps of her backpack from her and let it fall to the bed.

"This next" he said, tugging at her shirt. Obedient as ever, she stripped it off over her head. "Sit down." He pushed her back with enough force that she drew in her breath at the momentary uncertainty of falling. She caught herself and sat upright before him, in a pose so familiar to her it made her ache. Under her hand on the bed she felt his old quilt, and realized that was what carried his scent.

"Why are you so angry at me?" she whispered.

He spun away from her into the darkness. "I'm not mad at you!" His voice was broken and hollow, from somewhere across the room. Then suddenly he was before her, on his knees, his face close to hers. "When I see you, I see the life I could have had. The life I did have before all... this."

He grabbed her hips, pulling her to him as he buried his face between her breasts.

"You want my teeth or my cock?" he asked, his voice gruff with lust.

"I want you."

He groaned and pushed her back on the bed, running his hands over her breasts. Fingering the lace edging of her bra, he followed it under her arm; the mesh was frayed and gaping there. He undid the clasp. She sensed him watching her breasts slide to the side. As her nipples stiffened, they both knew it was not due to the chill air.

She lay there before him, her breath slow and even. Waiting as always for whatever he had to give her: flesh, leather, or steel. He ran his hand over the swell of her belly down to the gentle curve under her jeans. Tugging them down a bit he rested his cheek against her crotch. Madison knew he could smell her sweat, fear and musk.

"I can't. I can't do this". He pushed away from her. "Get out your gear and feed me."

He sat back on his haunches as she complied, feeling for her bag in the dark and pulling out a small flashlight. It illuminated her as she worked, opening a new syringe, lining up the vials on a clean cloth. Her breasts swayed softly in the shadows as she tied off the tourniquet on her arm. She felt his eyes, following the movement. Was he remembering their time together? As the blood began to rise, she knew the hunger would wipe out any other thoughts.

She filled the first vial, twisted it free and handed it to him without looking. She knew the eyes of a vampire as they fed and did not want to see him like that. He drained the flask and immediately tossed it on the bed. He didn't have to ask for more. After the third vial she began removing her gear, taped a cotton ball over the puncture and held her fingers against it. He sat still, his head bowed. Finally he reached forward and gently cupped her breasts, captured them in her bra, expertly closing it.

"I'll take you home," was all he said. By the time she reached her rooms she was dizzy and a pallid dawn touched the eastern sky.

"I can't make it back," he said.

"You can stay here" she said, opening the hall closet, a narrow walk-in. "There is no natural light here." She pulled out a comforter and laid it on the floor. Pushing past him in the closet doorway, she felt a rush of desire. He stopped her, cupped her face briefly, and then let her pass. As she closed the door he stammered, "I'm trusting you."

"I trusted you."

"Yeah, I'm still not convinced of the wisdom in that."

"I am," she whispered, and left him in darkness.

* * * *

He slept as best he could. Even though she was quiet, there were sounds and smells; the shower, grilled cheese, street noise, wet earth in a window box. Finally as night closed in, there were raised voices; hers, adamant, and a man, complaining. He recognized it as John, from the alley. "I just hope you know what you're doing!" Then a door slammed. *Of course she doesn't know what she is doing,* David thought. *She just let a bull of a vampire into her home.*

He heard her pause in the hall, and then she left as well. He felt the night coming down as he walked out into the living room. She had the same décor as always, an odd collection of thrift store finds and hand-me-downs. He picked up the pale blue porcelain poodle on the coffee table. "But I like the color" he could hear her explaining.

He entered her bedroom. A twin bed with a faded quilt left no room for a companion. Opening her closet, he found what he was looking for: her toy box, matte black metal, high on a shelf. In it he could visualize her leather cuffs and flogger, lovingly oiled, amid coils of hemp. He ran his hand over the box and drew away dust, frowning.

* * * *

Madison entered the apartment carrying her groceries just as he exited her bedroom. She didn't challenge his intrusion there, merely put the bag on the kitchen counter.

"How did you sleep?" she asked.

"Not well."

"I'm sorry, this is a noisy neighborhood."

"Your friend was here."

"He's not my friend—he's just a co-worker."

"He'd like to be your friend."

"Well, he isn't." She walked towards him. He was silhouetted against the twilight, his face in shadow, only his eyes—silvered.

"So who are you seeing?"

"No one."

"Why not?"

"I've been busy."

"No one is that busy."

She looked at the floor.

"I was waiting."

"For me."

She nodded.

"For two years."

She nodded again.

He put his hands on her shoulders and pulled her to him. She relaxed against his chest as he nuzzled her hair.

"I told you not to do that."

"I know. It's the only time I've ever disobeyed you."

"I don't think you should be punished for that." He cupped the sides of her face and tilted it towards his. "But I'm going to anyway."

She felt her womb contract and her hips go weak. He pressed his mouth to hers, softly at first. She could feel his teeth under his lips, hard.

He pulled away suddenly. "I have to go feed, for real. Last night was sweet, but I wasn't joking about needing a lot of blood."

He went to the window and opened it, noting the concrete balcony, the fire escape.

"Aren't you going to ask me about her? The blonde?"

"No."

He looked out at the sky, back at her, then out again. Weighing something or remembering something. She wondered which.

"She's the one who did this to me."

Then he was gone.

* * * *

When he returned it was after midnight and she was asleep in her tiny bed. He stood over her for a time, watching her breathe, the tiny shudders that ran through her body. Was she dreaming? Suddenly she opened her eyes. He drew the covers from her and casually ran his hand over her breasts and across her stomach. With a simple touch he parted her thighs, then abruptly turned and left the room. "Go back to sleep," he said over his shoulder.

* * * *

The next day she had to work late and did not get home before nightfall. Her day had been spent in frustrated fantasy, interrupted by requests for spreadsheets, quarterly numbers, and conference calls to distant lands. Meanwhile she was in a dream of firm bindings, soft touches, sharp punctures and exquisite pleasures.

As soon as she entered her apartment she knew it was empty. *Maybe he's gone out to feed*, she thought, and got her own dinner. Later she took down her toy box and saw the handprint on it. Opening it, she fingered the heavy pearl necklace that wound through the contents like a snake.

She remembered a time they had gone to dinner with his work friends. One of David's coworkers had gotten very drunk and asked her something. Later, back at his place, David had asked her, "What did Cory say to you? I saw him stop you in the hallway."

"He asked how much you were paying me to be with you." They were in the kitchen, surrounded by his cold green granite and copper. He looked her over, her simple black dress and long white strand of pearls.

"And what did you tell him?"

138

"I said I couldn't reveal the full amount, but it was in inches, not dollars." She smiled, feeling clever. His face had tightened as he looked at her, but was as ever inscrutable.

"Come here," he said. She'd approached him. "Turn around and face the counter." This was a time after he'd explained what was expected of her, and well before the introduction of rope and leather. There was a tickle in her lower belly, of desire, and of fear.

He unzipped her dress and let it fall to the floor. "Step out of it." She did as she was told and he pushed it away. He unhooked her bra and cast it aside. She felt cold and vulnerable standing under the lights with only her pearls, thigh-highs and flats.

She heard him taking off his tie, and then he grabbed her hands and bound them firmly behind her with it. She heard his zipper and the jangle of his trousers hitting the floor. He took her shoulders and positioned her next to the counter. Then he kicked lightly at her feet until she moved first one and then the other a good distance apart. David walked around the side of her and lifted her pearls. She thought he would take them off but instead he laid them on the counter and in the same motion pressed her down until her collarbone rested on cold stone, the pearls trailing out before her. Her breasts hung down into space. He lightly ran his hands over them.

"You aren't questioning me."

"No."

"Good."

She'd turned her head away from him and let her cheek rest on the counter. He moved around behind her and began stroking her ass lightly with his fingertips, then his palms, in slow circles. There would come a day where this was a prelude to a spanking, or more, but then she hadn't any idea what to expect.

Unseen by her, he'd unscrewed the cap on a bottle of walnut oil and poured some down length of his erect cock. After smoothing it along his shaft, he'd positioned the head against her already wet opening.

"So the question is, will you take a partial payment," he teased her by moving just the head in and out, "or will you take it... in full." He slid his entire length into her in one surging movement and she groaned.

"Both," she whispered, not knowing if it was a real question. It was. He fucked her with long deep strokes, then pulled out until just the head tormented her. Sometimes he entered her in increments, sometimes all at once. Her thighs quivered as she struggled to keep her balance.

Suddenly he withdrew, flipped the pearls from her neck, swung her around and down onto a cold metal chair. Her vulva made an embarrassing splat as she sat down. He held the top of her head in one hand and stroked himself with the other, until he'd left a creamy cascade all about her neck and décolleté. When he'd finished, he grabbed a large wooden spoon from the counter and slapped it against her mons in short, shallow strokes that stung. She felt the sweetness of an orgasm that turned sharp and sudden, jerking her hips.

She'd known what she must look like splayed out before him—her decorated flesh helplessly twitching with the pleasure he had inflicted on her. Finally he stopped and she looked up at him through tears, wanting, but not daring, to say "I love you".

He'd looked at her hard and said, "Anyone makes a crack like that to you again, you send them straight to me". As he bent forward to release her bonds her cheek grazed his wet cock. Even after all that had just happened, all she'd wanted to do was take it in her mouth.

Madison stood in her bedroom winding the pearls through trembling fingers, remembering. And though she waited, he never did come back that night, or the next, or the next. She was irritable and anxious. What if something had happened to him? Why would he come back and then leave again? What should she have done, or not done?

* * * *

On her volunteer night she saw John at the center. He slouched against a table, his perpetually disheveled brown curls nearly covering his dark eyes. When he saw her he jumped up so quickly he nearly knocked over the table.

"So, how's your houseguest?" His words bit into her.

"I don't have one." She refused to look at him.

"Oh, you came to your senses?"

"No! I mean he just isn't there." This was getting painful.

John looked at her steadily. "Madison, I read a study." She rolled her eyes. "No, listen to me." He put his hand on her shoulder. "I read a study where they took mice and gave them drugs, always in a certain enclosure they called "the drug room", until the mice were addicted. They monitored the mouse's brain waves. After a while, they stopped and took the mouse off the drugs for a while. When they put it back in that same enclosure, it instantly showed the same brain waves, even without the drugs."

"I'm not a mouse."

"No, but you are in the drug room."

She shrugged off his hand. "You don't know what you're talking about."

"I don't want to see you get hurt. I care about you."

"You don't 'care' about me, you want to fuck me!"

141

He backed away, his face red. "Well, it's better than what he wants to do to you!" he hissed.

Madison went out alone that night, finally stopping at a bench beside the river. During the day it was a place for office workers to eat hurried lunches, in the evening a place for lovers to tryst, after midnight, a place for those whose purposes were better suited to darkness. She gazed at the water, dully reflecting the lights of the city. Seconds before he touched her, she felt him, a rush of energy stronger than any river.

"You shouldn't be out here alone." His arms folded, he leaned against the back of the bench, his face against her ear.

"Well, now I'm not alone." She felt a release, of all sadness and tension. He was back, and that was all that mattered.

"I need to tell you about Amanda."

"Oh." She felt the tingle of apprehension in her belly. *No*, she thought, *I don't want to hear this.*

But she couldn't help herself. He talked. She listened, her arms folded tight under her breasts. He spoke of his first glimpse of Amanda at an exclusive club, long blonde hair, tight body encased in black leather. She was performing a suspension demonstration. Later she had performed the same acts on him – in private.

Madison felt her heart break at that. He had never let her restrain him, in any way. To be allowed to bind someone like him! She guessed she didn't measure up. How could the blonde earn a privilege in one night that she, in faithful service, couldn't secure in years?

It had been during one of those sessions that Amanda had turned him. David was helpless, and enraged. His first act had been to kill her. But it was too late then for anything more than vengeance. He could not return to

Madison in his new state as he had too little control and would have killed her, or worse.

"Why do you leave?" She had thought the words so often; it was startling to hear them coming out of her mouth. Immediately she regretted it. She felt pathetic. There was a long silence, broken only by the rush of the river.

"I don't know. I just start feeling... like I need to leave."

Suddenly she was angry. What did it matter if she displeased him? He would leave at some point no matter what she did. "You leave because you need to leave? What the hell kind of answer is that?" She stood and turned to face him, just a silhouette against the lights of the park.

"I'll always..." and he looked down at his feet. A boyish gesture she had never seen. "I'll always run away from you, Madison. And I don't know if I can spend eternity doing that."

"We don't have eternity."

"We could."

She didn't respond. The weight of those two words hung between them.

"I'm going home," she said at last. "You are welcome to join me if you like."

Back at her apartment she ignored him and got in the shower. It was getting towards dawn and he would be sleeping soon anyway.

She got out of the shower and walked into the living room, still toweling off. The shades were all drawn; the only light came from the kitchen. She could see him standing by the table. There was a wedge pillow on it, draped with her purple throw. Her ropes coiled at either side. He was naked. She dropped her towel and approached him.

"Still haven't punished you for disobeying me."

She was silent, standing before him with her feet together, hands folded before her, head slightly bowed.

He raised her chin with a finger; she was unable to meet his eyes. "Look at me." She did. They stood with their gaze locked until she trembled in a nakedness that had nothing to do with her lack of clothing.

He placed her on the table, leaned her back against the pillow. Lifting her left leg, he bent it at the knee, then slipped a loop of rope over her left wrist and began binding her forearm to her thigh. He worked slowly and skillfully, creating firm, even wraps. She did not take her eyes off his face. He bound the right arm and leg in the same way, until she was spread open before him. He stood back and looked at her. She could imagine what he saw. Her rapt face, breasts upturned, her open and wet labia framed so beautifully with his handiwork. He moved over her and kissed her mouth very softly.

"Close your eyes," he said. And she did. She could hear nothing for a very long time and then the swish and brush of air across the skin of her belly. She jerked involuntarily.

"Hmm... you *are* out of practice, aren't you?" He gently stroked the flogger across her neck and shoulders, around and over her breasts, down her flanks and all over her tummy. It flickered across the tender moons of flesh under the back of her thighs where they met her buttocks. He let it tickle her smooth mons until she shivered. Then he stopped and waited. She felt the rush of air before the lashes kissed the erect flesh of her left nipple. She did not move or flinch. He moved methodically from her left to her right and back with short shallow strokes. Then he moved slowly across and down her body as her hips began to tremble.

When he reached her pubic area, he began stroking the leather down the hinge of her thigh. Finally he dangled the lashes over her clit.

"I was never very good at punishing you, was I?" She was silent. Then he whipped the flogger down on her clit and sent her jerking into an orgasm that left her shaking, with tears streaming down her cheeks.

"Look at me."

Madison opened her eyes. For a moment she felt everything was as it had been before, before the blonde, before his change. She thought her heart would break. At that instant he entered her, surging forward, over her, his face near hers, his mouth on hers, then against her neck. She felt the sharpness of his teeth. Then there was blood, so much blood. Something she couldn't understand.

David was still stretched over her. Cold blood flooded into her face, her neck, her hair. John's grinning visage loomed over what was left of David's ruined neck, triumphant, a steel blade in his hand. And then there was light, blazing all around her, as John yanked down the curtains. John who had entered via the very means she had left open for her lover, the window, the fire escape. And then came the ash, exploding, drifting, coating her in a layer as soft and fine as body powder.

John approached her, a look of disgust on his face. He brought the blade down. She thought he meant to kill her too but instead he began slicing at the rope. It was then she found her voice, screaming at him.

"Stop, please stop!" She wanted, needed the rope—that was the last thing David had done for her. John ignored her pleas.

Loosed from her bonds, she tumbled from the table. John was gone. She lay on the floor where she fell, naked in the cold light, wearing nothing but ash.

* * * *

The New Normal
© Jay Lygon

Sarajevo, 1993

Pazite, Snajper! (Beware, Sniper!)

Sniper Alley wasn't the name of this street when I lived here. That pile of rubble was my apartment, an old building with ten units above the café where Zoran argued passionately about religion, magic, and philosophy over tiny cups of syrupy coffee. No less passionately, but without his purity, I stared his mouth. It was as if all the color in his face pooled in his wide lips. When he caught me staring, pink blotches would appear on his cheeks. Eyelashes any girl would have killed for fluttered as he stared at his tapping fingers. If we were drunk enough, I'd lunge across the table to kiss him.

He'd push me back and laugh. "You're drunk, Dusan."

He was never drunk enough.

* * * *

Or maybe this pile of blasted bricks and twisted rebar was the shoe shop and that pile was the café. Without the green awning it's hard to remember. My memories were fading. Ten years ago, during the Olympics, the world was in love with Sarajevo, but they'd since forgotten it existed. The Serbian artillery in the hills surrounding us would soon make sure there was nothing left to remember.

People were harder to forget, but they were difficult to remember accurately too. They shifted in the mind, becoming more than they were—more kind, more saintly—while the truth of them faded. Even Zoran, who filled my masturbation fantasies while we were at university, had dissolved to little more than an eternally young, beautiful boy without distinct features other than his mouth.

I shoved my hands in my jeans pockets and kicked the edge of the plywood sign leaning against a tower of broken bricks. With my enhanced vision, I could see the streaks of blue paint that ran under each letter of the sniper warning even in the dark. I wondered if the residents needed to be reminded that random death awaited them in the streets. Maybe some strolled a little slower as they passed the sign in the hopes that today was the day the sniper got them. Everyone had a breaking point.

Mine came when I saw death stalking the bushes in the no man's land between Serb and Croat neighborhoods where men still gathered. I grabbed him by the gold chain tangled in his chest hair and forced his teeth into my neck. The miserable bastard refused to finish me off. Never trust a Serbian, even if he has a huge cock.

Why did I go back to my old neighborhood? Misery might have loved company, but I didn't have to go there to find it; it was everywhere in the city. Maybe I was in search of my humanity. Like my old apartment building though, I was sure it had been destroyed. The siege had a way of prying it out of even the most tenacious grasp.

"Dusan? Is that you?" The harsh whisper carried from the dark doorway of an apartment building several feet away from the ruins where I stood. Bullet holes pockmarked the façade. Garbage that would never be collected sat in a pile in the gutter. "Come out of the street! Quickly!"

The more he spoke, the more sure I was that he was Zoran. Hope and doubt flooded through me. I flinched back then chuckled at myself for fearing a ghost. In the hierarchy of monsters, phantasms meant nothing. They were mere memories, after all, and memories were so fragile.

I went to the doorway, but of course could not enter. That lanky shadow could only be Zoran.

"Is that really you, Dusan? You're alive?" Clearly, he doubted.

"I'm not exactly dead." Truth might have been be the first causality of war, but sometimes it refused to go gently into that good night—until some politician staked it through the heart. Like me, my version of the truth had one foot in the grave.

"You'll be shot if you stand out in the open. It's too dark to see the sniper warning, but this street is dangerous. Come inside, please."

Zoran was still a foolish boy. Didn't he think about where he was standing? After all, he was the one who studied folktales and myths at university. Back then I hadn't understood how important that knowledge could be in the modern world, but since things had changed, I could have told him how the doorframe—splintered as it was—protected him from things far worse than snipers. The threshold was a place of powerful magic that divided the realm of the supernatural from the human. Two years ago, such an idea would have seemed laughably medieval, but conditions in Sarajevo had spun back to that point in time. Electricity and peace were the new fairytales.

The threshold was also the symbol of the body, inviolate. The old sicknesses could still kill you, as there were no hospitals or doctors left to speak of, but there were new diseases out there that were worse. Invite anyone to come inside at your peril. And yet, he pleaded with me.

Inside the foyer, Zoran immediately grasped me in the embrace I'd long dreamed of, but with a different sort of passion. I closed my eyes and wished the desperation was

148

lust, not fear. With stiff arms, I hugged him back and murmured words of comfort. Yes, it's me. No, I'm not a ghost. I'm sorry I didn't say goodbye. Yes, I missed you.

He pulled back to shake my hand and kiss my cheeks three times. His face wasn't exactly as I'd remembered it. It was more gaunt than before, and his brown eyes had lost some of their puppy dog openness. He tried to glance away from my stare, but couldn't. He shouldn't have looked into my eyes. I could have held him there forever. I could have compelled him to do things with his mouth that he'd only done in my fantasies.

That was an old hunger. It gnawed at me when I'd had my fill of blood and the rest of the night stretched before me. Regret was a terrible thing when it seemed it could haunt me for all eternity. Sentiment, or more likely pride, stopped me from commanding him to his knees, but I still took a kiss. Like the old days, he laughed and pulled away, but he didn't push. Instead, he grasped my arm. A ropey blue vein crossed the back of his hand to his knuckle. It twitched with his pulse. Before my hungers overwhelmed me, I had to look away.

The foyer walls met at odd angles. Some artillery blast, maybe the one that destroyed my apartment, had knocked his building sideways. It made me feel as if I were falling even though I knew I wasn't.

"Come on upstairs. Everyone will be so glad to see you again." Zoran bounded halfway up the staircase before stopping to look over his shoulder at me. It was if we were in a different time, before the siege began, when we'd staggered into this foyer late at night. He'd jog up the stairs, sure I was behind him, while I held back and wondered if I could stand to watch him turn into someone else for his family. Reluctantly, then and now, I followed.

His butt flexed under his jeans, a mesmerizing sight as I followed it up the three flights to his family's apartment. At the landing, he said, "You look hungry," and I tried not to laugh. Did he have any idea what he was saying?

A bare bulb left the furthest doors in the hallway in shadow. The carpet had worn through in spots. The building's list was more pronounced up there, and I put a hand on a wall to steady myself, but immediately pulled it back from the greasy wallpaper.

Zoran opened his apartment door. Bright light made me recoil. "Look who I brought!" he said to someone inside.

I thought about running, but didn't.

* * * *

His parent's apartment was still a claustrophobic mash of cabbage rose sofas and lace doilies. I stood by the cabinet of green cut glass goblets and tried to sort through the overwhelming rush of odors and noise. Zoran shut the door and pulled me deeper into the room.

Oil lamps burned at every table. That explained the coating on the wallpaper. Where they got the kerosene was a wonder. I hadn't seen that much light during night hours since the university library burned down.

"It's Dusan! He was standing out in the middle of the street." He lightly punched my arm.

Zoran's sister sat at the dining table, books spread before her. Chewing on the end of a pen, she stared at me with harsh brown eyes. Her thoughts couldn't have been more transparent. She had always been a frighteningly practical girl, and I probably struck her as the proverbial last man on earth. Thankfully, she decided I wasn't worth her time and leaned back over her books.

His father glanced at me around a yellowing newspaper and grunted.

150

"Dusan, you naughty boy. Where have you been?" Zoran's mother grabbed me and placed wet kisses on my cheeks. "You're so cold. Sit, sit. Coffee?"

Instead of wiping away her kiss, I took a seat. "You have coffee?"

I tried to figure out how to talk without showing my fangs. Hiding behind my hand would only work for so long. Even if she'd seen them though, we both knew who was the most powerful creature in that room. Her eyebrow arched as she placed a cup in front of me. When I didn't move, she pushed the sugar bowl across the table. What else could I do but accept her hospitality?

Every eye was on the spoon I lifted from the bowl. The three humans held their breath. I shook some of the sugar off the spoon, then more, and finally most of it until someone exhaled.

The coffee reeked of burned beans. It tasted worse. Still, I smiled with my lips pursed tightly together and sighed as I relaxed back into the chair. Finally, the others stopped staring. Zoran sat beside me and rocked back on his chair.

"Sit like a civilized man." His mother set coffee in front of him and lightly smacked the back of his head. Then she sat down with her own cup. She leaned forward, eyes sharp. "We thought you were dead, Dusan."

"So many people are nowadays."

"Why didn't you come visit? Zoran missed you."

"Did he?"

Zoran scratched his chest when I glanced at him. His sister snorted. It made me stupidly happy to imagine he'd said that.

"Where have you been hiding yourself?"

How could I have forgotten his mother's interrogations? "Around."

151

"Around, he says. Why do you boys always have to be so mysterious? Where does Zoran go at night? Around, he says too."

Also wondering where Zoran went at night, I turned to look at him. He squirmed. I kept staring. He lifted his coffee cup to his lips so that his mother couldn't see his mouth when he whispered, "Later."

She slapped her hand on the table, making our spoons clatter against the saucers. "One day, he'll disappear, and when I ask the police to find him, they'll say, 'Where was he last?' and I'll say, 'Around.'"

More likely the police would take her to one of the morgues and leave her to wander through the sacks of bodies.

Still clucking, she bustled to the kitchen and brought out her famous *savijaca* pastry. Zoran's father folded his newspaper. His sister pushed aside her books as his mother put the sweet cheese strudel in front of me. They watched me cut off a piece that was big enough to satisfy their honor, but not so much that they'd call me greedy. Then they helped themselves.

The coffee and food warred with my stomach. I pushed back from the table and mumbled about the water closet as I stumbled out of the room. So that they wouldn't hear me retching, I turned on the faucet full blast. There I was, the big, bad monster, brought to my knees by coffee and strudel.

After washing my face, I went back to the cluttered room. The tilted walls made me dizzy. The air was so thick that it was an effort to move through it. Not thinking, I went to the window and drew back the drapes to let in fresh air. Where the glass had been, there was a sheet of plywood covered by a poster so that from a distance it looked as if they still had a view of the outside. Of course they wouldn't allow any light from their oil lamps to shine through a window. That would be like sending coordinates to the Serbian artillery.

"I took that picture," his sister said as I stared at the poster. Her wide, pink mouth spread into an expectant smile as she waited for her compliment.

"It's very nice."

It was horrible, a mockery of the ruins outside. The picture had been taken from the window where I stood, but on a sunny day, when there had been people on the street, before the siege began. I'd forgotten about the small post office. Like the leaning walls of their building, the picture made me stomach lurch. I drew the curtain and plopped back into my chair.

As they drank their coffee, Zoran casually spoke of taking a holiday at a lake outside the city with some girls who may or may not have existed. No one asked him how he planned to get there, or why he thought the Serbs would let him merrily traipse past their lines on his way to the lake. His sister and mother chatted about school and fashion. Zoran's father complained about politicians. It was as if the real world didn't exist for his family. They were either valiant or insane.

Under the table, Zoran squeezed my knee. He nodded toward the door. I started making goodbye noises. That set his mother into a frenzy. She offered me more coffee and dinner. Fortunately, my excuses met only as much protest as good manners called for. Otherwise, they were probably glad to see me go—not because they guessed I was vampire, but because I'd drank their coffee and ate their food and then had been rude enough to puke it up.

Zoran said something about escorting me home. No one pointed out that my old home was the weed-choked field next door, or that he didn't know where my new place was. His mother kissed me again. I tried not to think about her rich, thick, juicy blood. His sister and father had returned to their reading and didn't look up to see my feeble wave goodbye.

Out in the hallway, Zoran rolled his eyes. "Sorry about that."

"Then why did you take me to them?" I asked as we walked shoulder to shoulder down the dark stairs.

He shrugged. "We're starved for new blood. No one visits anymore. It's the same old conversation every night. 'Where are you going, Zoran? Why do you go out at night?' It's driving me mad."

"Where do you go at night? Were you headed out when you saw me?"

He'd stopped on the stairs before I did. I heard his breath catch. "There's a park..."

There were hundreds of parks in Sarajevo, but I knew instantly which one he meant. "Stay away from that place. It's dangerous."

His laughter had a bitter, knowing edge to it that I'd never heard before. How infuriating to think he'd been giving himself to men all along when I could barely get a kiss from him. Feeling the fool, I stomped down the stairs. He grabbed my arm.

"Don't be angry. You've obviously been there too."

That was different.

He put his arm across my shoulders. "Come with me to the park. We can hunt together. I'm so horny tonight, I don't care who sucks my cock."

In a daze, I let him lead me out of the building and onto the street.

* * * *

Ordinarily, I would have heard the bullet long before it threatened me, but I was sunk in blue thoughts, so I didn't until it hit the *Beware! Sniper!* sign and splintered the wood. Zoran grabbed my arm and pulled me across the ruins of my old apartment to a high pile of bricks. We dodged behind it.

For a moment, I almost hoped Zoran was hit. I could have saved his life by turning him. He would have been grateful. In my wild imagination, it was all very dramatic and romantic—for a few seconds before I realized I sickened myself. I was a monster, but had yet to sink into being monstrous.

Zoran peered around the rubble. "They don't usually shoot at night. Maybe the Serbian army gave him night goggles."

Another bullet struck the ground near us. I pulled him back to safety.

"He knows we're here. I guess we just have to wait him out." Zoran rubbed his hands down his lean thighs. "Oh well. So, where did you disappear to? You seem to be doing all right. You're not starving."

Adopting a mysterious air, I told him "I've been keeping out of sight, mostly. Just trying to survive, like anyone else."

"You're a smuggler, aren't you?"

It was my heart overriding my common sense, but at that moment, he seemed to be the way I remembered him. His eyes were huge and sincere in the darkness, full of the worship I'd always wanted to see. Maybe it was wrong to lie, but I wanted him to think I was cunning enough to sneak through the Serbian forces in the hills around Sarajevo, and brave enough to come back with the supplies that kept our people alive, so I nodded.

He grabbed his crotch as he leaned over to peer around the rubble again. "God, I'm so horny."

"Being shot at turns you on?"

Chuckling, he stroked himself through his jeans. "Makes you understand that life is too short for regrets."

"Funny, I was thinking almost the same thing earlier."

He crawled to me, his knees scraping on the rough ground. "I know what you regret." His mouth pressed against mine. When his tongue tried to push past my lips, I jerked back and hit my head on the pile of rubble.

"What's the matter, Dusan?"

What if my mouth tasted like old blood? Or if he noticed my fangs?

"I see. You want more than a kiss."

Yes, I did. I always had. What I truly wanted I could never have though, because the moment his cock entered my mouth or ass, he'd feel how cool my body was, and then he'd know I wasn't alive, and be terrified, or disgusted.

He sat back on his heels. "So, what do you like?"

What I liked were memories of him at the café, where he'd been more alive than anywhere else. Even though we'd never been to the lake together, I could imagine him diving expertly into the frigid water, and then wading out, water streaming from his hair, sunlight glistening on his skin, his swimsuit clinging to the outline of his cock.

"Who would have thought you'd be the shy one? Come on, Dusan, don't leave me like this." He reached for the top button of my jeans.

If my heart still beat, it would have pounded out of my chest as I watched him reach into my fly and take out my cock. He grinned and bent down. Those lips slid down, sucking gently as he left a trail of spit behind. Then he took me into his mouth, plunging my cock into warmth. He bobbed too fast, as if trying to get me off in a hurry, so I put my hand on his head. Even his hair was warm.

He fumbled with his pants and started stroking himself.

The gravel and broken glass poked my back as I slid down to suck him off. He knelt with his knees pressed to my head and he tried to ram down my throat. When he bent over me to take my cock back into his mouth, he pumped me with his hand.

"Slow down," I whispered.

"There are snipers out here."

"I know places we can go and take our time."

He sped up. My cock was banging against his teeth and he kept catching my pubes as he slammed his fist up and down.

Hoping to teach by example, I grabbed his hips to stop him from shoving his cock down my throat. He hadn't noticed my mouth was cold. I eased back his foreskin and ran my tongue around the exposed area. His head stopped bobbing for a second. My tongue slid over his balls. The vibration of his groan surrounded my cock.

Zoran kept trying to shove into my mouth, but he was no match for my strength. I could hold him above me all night, and he'd just have to let me take my time. When I finally took him in, I lifted my head off the ground and worked tight lips down his shaft until my nose was in his crotch. I took my time breathing in the smell of him. Too bad he'd bathed recently. I hated the taste of lavender.

His thighs flexed as he tried to take back control, but I'd had years to dream about it and there was no way I'd rush my moment. Except for the occasional pump or lick, he'd stopped paying attention to my cock. I flipped him onto the ground. His cock pointed up, with a slight turn to the left. I grasped his ass with both hands and lifted him up my mouth. He started to say something, but his eyes met my gaze.

"Quiet. There are snipers," I told him.

His beautiful mouth hung open as he nodded. I kept a lock on his gaze as I worked my tongue down his shaft to his balls again. Each long, slow lick made him twitch. His head was dark purple, almost busting with blood and so tempting to taste, but I couldn't bring myself to bite him there.

Zoran's hands slid down his thighs and clenched into fists. I lost control over him as his eyes fluttered closed. He grabbed my hair and thrust into my mouth until he tensed. Then he pulled out and shot onto my lips. I leaned over him, spreading his load over his mouth. That was the best part, our lips sliding together, his come smeared between us as we pushed it back and forth between our mouths.

"Fuck. Jesus." His arm stretched over his head as he sprawled on the ground. "Wow." Then he made a tired gesture at my cock. "Sorry, um..."

"It's okay."

He glanced up at the sky and shoved his cock into his jeans. "Well, okay. Good. Do you think the sniper is gone?"

"I have no idea."

He sat up. "I guess I can sneak around this side of my building and go up the back staircase." As he dusted off his shirt, he shot a glance at me. "Can you get home okay?"

"Don't worry about me."

"Good." He leaned over and quickly kissed me. "Next time, I'll get you off, I swear." He stood in a crouch and peered around the pile of rubble. Looking over his shoulder at me, he flashed a grin. "Bring sugar next time. Or coffee. But sugar is better."

My forehead furrowed.

"You're a smuggler, right? So bring me something."

At that moment, I saw how much he looked like his sister.

"Don't forget."

Crunching gravel and the slide of his feet across the uneven ground allowed me to listen to his escape even though I couldn't bear to watch him.

I thought about the sniper as I sat behind the rubble for another hour or so. Theoretically, I could have figured out the angle of his shots and traced back to his position. Killing him would have been easy. But I had no good reason to do it. As monsters went, he was a nothing. That made me laugh. If the sniper was a nothing, how low did that make Zoran? Or maybe it only made him human.

What right did I have to be bitter? If I'd chosen to remember him as different from the way he truly was, whose fault was that? Mine alone.

I stood. Thumbs hooked into my pockets, I glanced around the ruins and shrugged. The sniper was probably once a baker. I had been a student of philosophy, but became an undead blood sucker. And Zoran had once been someone I thought I knew, but was now whoring himself for sugar. The past was past, though, and we all had to accept the way things were. This was the new normal.

* * * *

Cat
© Giselle Renarde

I have no specific recollection of how Cat came into my life. One day she was just there, lying on my bed. She seemed to know me, I seemed to know her, and after one of the longest dry spells known to dykedom, that was good enough.

"Come to bed," she purred. She always seemed to be purring. Maybe that's why she was called *Cat*. I couldn't remember if it was a nickname or a diminutive of Cathleen or Catalina or something. At that point I was too embarrassed to ask. I was supposed to know her. The way she talked it seemed like she'd been in my bed for ages, and I was only just waking up to her.

"Look at the time," Cat said. She drew open the bed sheets, inviting me in. Had I ever seen her in that cotton cami or those little ruffled boy shorts? Everything about her—even her clothes—seemed hazily familiar, like I knew them from a dream. "Come on," she begged, with a pretty pout on her pink lips. "It's late."

"Late? It's only two." I felt like she ought to know I didn't consider two in the morning *late*, but at the same I didn't really know what she knew. "I work better at night," I explained, but that didn't seem relevant to her.

"You shouldn't stay up sketching all night," she teased. Her voice had the warmth of a cashmere blanket. When she spoke, I wanted to wrap myself in her words. "Do you want to turn into a vampire or something?"

The innocence of her tone made me chuckle. "Yup, that's it," I said. "All artists want to be vampires. That's why we work under the cover of darkness."

"Oh." She stretched out like a tabby. The way she looked at me, with total honesty, made me wonder if she didn't take me a little too seriously. But when she raised her eyebrows and crossed her long legs like a pin-up model, work was the last thing on my mind.

Setting down my pencil, I crawled on top of her and nuzzled in. Somehow I knew she'd giggle. As I kissed up and down her neck, she laughed so loudly I'm sure my neighbours thought they were in on our joke. "Suck my neck," she cried. Loudly. Her lithe body writhed beneath me. "Bite me!"

I wrapped my lips over my teeth like a toothless granny and chomped on her neck. She giggled so hard I thought she was going to die. I loved that something so simple evoked such a huge reaction. "Stop, stop," she wheezed between sputters of laughter. "Stop, I can't breathe!"

Showing mercy, I leaned away for a second. Her chest heaved as she sighed, giggled, sighed, giggled, her pixie face framed with messy orange curls. The weathered cotton of her cami was so sheer I could see her pink nipples forming tight buds underneath as her breathing regulated. A surge of electricity shot through me. I barely knew who she was, but I knew I couldn't resist her.

Pulling her top up over her head, I dove at her white little tits and sucked her hard nipples. They were like candy on my tongue. I loved her tits. If I had two heads, I'd have sucked them both at once. She ran her hands through my hair, moving my mouth from breast to breast as I thrust my hand beneath her shorts. Her slit was wet and waiting. When my fingers dove inside, she sighed and grasped my hair in her little fists. If I sucked hard, I could get her whole tit in my mouth, but she seemed more interested in the finger fucking.

"I want to take this the next level," she panted. In my books that meant fisting, but as I prepared to give her another finger she let go of my hair and rolled onto her belly.

I gasped as she fished through my night table. "Your back!" Why did her back come as such a shock when her clothes and her lips and her hair seemed so familiar? Had I never seen it before? Had she never rolled over naked in my bed?

Looking up at me, her eyes wide with alarm, she asked, "What's wrong?"

My head seemed to be shaking of its own volition. My whole body felt prickly and hot. I was horrified. Or was I fascinated? Maybe both. I was transfixed, at any rate. Her back was carved up like...well, really, the only comparison I could draw was, "You've got a back like a bathroom wall!"

A cheeky grin bled across her lips. "I like that," she said. "*A back like a bathroom wall.* I've never thought of it that way."

"Who did this to you?" I asked, though it was obviously more than one person. There were different names, different phone numbers, quotes and political messages, different styles of handwriting. Was it still considered *writing* when it was carved into a girl's back?

"Some people get tattoos every time they think they're in love," Cat reasoned. Her tone was dreamy and casual. She turned her head until her chin rested on her left shoulder, and pointed to the name there. "The first girl I slept with was Roxanne. I thought I was in love with her."

All I could do was stare. I didn't want to touch it—I didn't want to hurt her—but I wanted to know how her scars would feel against my skin. "And this was her idea of a tattoo?" I asked, tracing the big 'x' in the name with my fingertip.

"No, that was her idea of *love*," Cat replied. She shuddered as I stroked it. Her scar was the softest skin I'd ever touched. "Love and possession were the same thing to Roxanne. She sat on my back. She wasn't big, but she had some serious muscle to her. She sat with her ass in the curve of my back and her knees pressing my arms into her carpet, and she pulled this knife out of her pocket."

Fishing around in the drawer of my night table, she finally found what she was looking for: a razor-sharp scalpel with a shiny metal grip. When she passed the knife to me, I was surprised by its weight in my hand. "She took her time marking me with it. She dragged the knife through my skin and I could feel it cutting through me. Just one straight line to start the 'R.' I could feel that I was bleeding, but she leaned down and drank up every drop. No good wasting it on the carpet, she said. She did another line and drank the blood from that one, but then she said that was enough for one night..."

"For one night?" I stammered, shaking my head. I wouldn't have believed it if I didn't have my finger on the very 'R' she was talking about.

"Yes," Cat replied with a simple nod. "And I promised to stay with her until she'd finished putting her name in my skin. We did a little more each time. She'd lick my pussy or fuck me with her fingers, and then as the grand finale, she'd carve me up. We never lost a drop of blood to the carpet."

"What?" The word came out more explosively than I'd intended. I didn't want to seem judgmental, but it was all just crazy, wasn't it?

Handing me the scalpel, Cat giggled, "The bathroom wall wasn't built in a day. It's taken years to get to this point."

With a combination of nausea and awe, I traced my finger down from *Roxanne*, through a phone number with an international area code, and the words *Art is Life*. There were more names than I could stand to read.

Though I felt no sense of ownership over Cat, it hurt me to think of her with all those other people. I wouldn't let myself count how many names had stained her back with blood. Too many. But the worst part was that mine wasn't one of them. I looked down at the scalpel in my hand, *The next person to hold this thing will never know I was here.* I had to leave my mark.

Cat rested her head on my pillow. She wasn't looking at me when she asked, "Do you want to add your name to the bathroom wall?"

"Yes," I replied before she'd even finished speaking.

The biggest space I could find was down in her lower back, nearly along her side. Anywhere else, I'd have to condense my name to a diminutive, but I felt like if I was going ahead with this I might as well carve *Marjane* out in full.

My heart raced as I visualized the knife cutting the first line of the 'M'. I traced the scalpel through the air, imagining exactly what that line would look like: mostly straight, with a slight curve at the bottom.

"Remember to catch my blood after you make the cut," Cat called as I leaned in to put scalpel to skin. "Best way is with your tongue. Just suck it up. It'll heal faster, too."

"Okay," I agreed, leaning in very close. I rested the point of the scalpel millimeters away from her flesh and held that position so long my hand started to cramp. *What was I waiting for?* Pressing the tip of the knife into her skin, I drew it down, around, and out in one swift motion.

Cat shrieked in what sounded like half pain and half orgasm. I licked the line of blood tumbling down her flesh. The moment that thick metallic redness met my tongue, I knew I could never go back. Those few drops of sweet blood seemed to course through my veins, warming my toes and exploding like a supernova in my pussy. I gasped at the sensation her life force generated in me.

164

Setting the scalpel on my night table, I flipped her onto her side and grabbed at her tits as I licked the incision. I felt like an animal. Her blood made me wild. As I sucked the blood from her body, my throbbing clit drove me to grind against anything close by—and that *anything* ended up being her smoothly-shaven leg. I suckled her side. She nourished me. Her blood ran hot through my body, and I knew if I didn't get to feel her wet pussy on mine I would lose my mind.

In one swift motion, I tore off Cat's shorts and pressed them against the bleeding line in her side. Her legs were long, but her body was easy to manipulate. When I tucked my body neatly between her legs, she sighed, *Oh, Mari, Mari, Mari*, and my lungs just about exploded. Her voice contained all the passion of the willingly seduced.

Cat threw her leg over my shoulder. I kissed it, leaving a path of red as I sank into the V of her thighs. She pressed her wet pussy against mine, and I pressed back against her moist folds. Together, we were *juice*. We were one big pool of pussy juice lapping like waves against distant shores. The pressure of her wet lips on mine drove me wild. My body burned with her blood.

Neighbours be damned. I cried out in ecstasy of blood and sweat as my soul blazed. Cat was shouting too, screaming incomprehensible niceties as she circled her hips to press against me. We were stuck pussy to pussy, bound together in a writhing mass of bodies that seemed more than the two we were. As I lay face-up on my bed with a strange girl between my legs, I felt a sense of invigoration attached to my post-coital exhaustion.

"I can't believe I licked your blood," I said, shaking my head in amazement. It occurred to me I should clean her wound with something more than my tongue, but when I lifted her little cotton shorts from her side there was nothing there but a clean cut in her flesh. No blood. I stared in disbelief. "I cut you. You bled. Why aren't you bleeding now?"

Cuddling her head on my pillow, she giggled. "I told you your tongue would seal it up." Her eyes seemed to melt from sky blue to sea foam green as she held my gaze. "How did it taste?"

"Good," I said. I could still taste the metallic sweetness of her blood on my lips. When I licked them, all her strength surged through me. "It tastes incredible, actually."

So incredible that I began to crave not only its taste but also the surge of fiery power that coursed through my body with every lick. Each night I carved a new line. I sucked the blood from her fresh wound. She gave herself over to me. When I looked at her back, I didn't see a bathroom wall anymore. I saw generosity of spirit. Cat was the most benevolent creature I'd ever known.

It would take twenty-three nights, I estimated, to spell out 'Marjane' all in capital letters.

"What are you?" I asked on that final evening. Only the last line of my 'E' remained to be carved. As I sketched her, I could only think how *normal* she looked. She couldn't be human, could she? *Was I?* At one time yes, but not anymore. I could feel the change in my body and my cravings.

"I told you when we met," she said with a smile, like she was amused by my forgetfulness. "I told you who I am."

My pencil scratched against the paper as I shaded her inner thighs. That night, she wore a satin slip that barely covered her hips when she lay on her side. I licked my lips. Sex and blood were becoming one in my mind. Cat had everything I wanted. "I don't remember," I finally confessed. I hoped she wouldn't be upset.

With a quaint chuckle, she said, "I'm the Catalyst. You wanted to switch your days to nights. You wanted to give your life over to art. I am *the way*. I'm the means to that end."

I didn't understand, and that's what I told her, though I suspected if I'd concentrated more on the conversation and less on my art I might have figured it out on my own. As much as I wanted to put down my pencil, I couldn't do it until I'd finished her portrait. It was the only way for me to keep her, in any sense.

"Haven't you ever heard that art is life?" she giggled. I couldn't get over how coy she was with me, even though she was living in my bed.

"Sure," I said, still putting pencil to paper. "It's carved into your back—*Art is Life.*"

"You want to be a true artist," she replied, tracing her big toe up the back of the opposite calf. "Where do you suppose all that life force comes from? If it came from you, your art would eat you alive. You'd be dead in a day. If you want to create like the masters, you have to live like them." Taking the scalpel from my night table, she held it up like an instrument of worship. "I've given you a taste. Now you have the blood lust. I've been your mother and suckled you with my life, but after tonight you'll be on your own to procure your meals. Do you think you can handle that?"

My pencil fell from my hand. "No," I said. My head seemed to be shaking. I couldn't stop it, even as I dropped my sketch and ran to join her on my bed. "You're my source, Cat. If you leave me, I'll die of thirst."

Leaning forward, she ran her fingers through my hair and planted a sweet kiss on my forehead. "You can fly, baby bird," she assured me. "I know you'll figure it out."

"No, I really won't." I was starting to panic, but her smile reassured me.

"Where's your confidence gone?" she asked. "You're more innovative than you know, so don't go asking me where your next meal is coming from. I can only tell you where to get your *last supper*." She cocked her eyebrow as she handed me the scalpel. "Finish the E."

The instrument had never felt so heavy in my hand. I suppose I must have known all along my ginger Cat was initiating me into another realm of existence, but I hadn't counted on her leaving until I was ready to let her go. Now the end was drawing near and all I could do was cut.

She sighed into my pillow as I traced the knife through her flesh. The sensation of cutting deep into her skin was familiar to me now, but no less invigorating. After a brief moment of molecular shock, small drops of red rose to the surface. My legs quivered even though I was sitting. My heart seemed to beat in double time. I licked my lips.

Tossing the scalpel to the night table, I threw my face at her side and savored the taste. Her blood ran through me as I sucked it from her body. Its sweetness filled my cheeks and its warmth burned inside me. She sighed at the sensation, but I knew how nice she'd feel if I pressed my palm against her pussy.

Cat seized, tossing her head back on my pillow. As I squeezed her pussy lips together, she moaned my name, *Marjane*, and pressed her thighs tight around my hand. I stroked her gorgeous slit. Her juice soaked my bare fingers while her blood drenched my lips. When she reached under my top and grabbed my tits, I sucked her side with renewed vigor. Her soft hands felt incredible against my skin. *Why did she have to leave?* She squeezed my breasts as I lapped her blood in ecstasy. *Why couldn't she stay with me? Nourish me? Feed me?*

My hand went wild on her slippery clit and she threw her head to the side, pinching my nipple hard. Her sweet blood coated my lips when she came loud as ever. She was pain and she was joy. Her scream was the cry of an infant entering this world with the wisdom of the ages. She gave me all.

How can I describe Cat but to say she was my creator and my creation? She was the Catalyst who sparked my blood lust. She was my artist's enabler. Without her, what would I be? *Normal?* What artist could live that way? *Normality, mediocrity*—artists cringe at these words.

I don't remember Cat leaving. Of course, I didn't remember her coming either. In and out like a lamb, but a lion in the interim. I understood why she had to leave. There were others like me, other artists fated to add their names to her bathroom wall. She had to tend to them all, and there was only one of her. In that sense, I marvel at the number of weeks she devoted to my personal catalysis.

The taste of her sweet blood planted a longing in my veins, but I'm on my own now, fending for myself. It's as sexually charged as you can imagine, but not as challenging as I'd anticipated. You'd be surprised how many backs are out there, just waiting to be scratched.

* * * *

Lisabet Sarai, editor

One More Transformation
© Nobilis Reed

We started with a tour of the extra-national platform. Frjálsræði was larger than I expected, extending a hundred meters into the sky, and a hundred more under the ocean surface. At the very top were the satellite receivers and the docking station for the airship that brought me. We descended through the tower, visiting living quarters and recreational facilities, server rooms and workstations for the data wranglers who brought in much of the platform's money. Below that were manufacturing facilities and laboratories, and then deep under the water, facilities associated with the platform's fishery. It was mildly interesting but not what I had come for. It was a ritual, designed to impress us.

There were just four of us, the only ones who would arrive for the procedure this month. The others were like me, senior executives from prestigious corporations. None of them were from my own company, nor did they represent any of my firm's rivals; no doubt the invitations had been carefully arranged to make sure that inter-corporate disagreements didn't become a problem.

My transformation could only be accomplished at this kind of place. Any of the nation-states, the ones burdened by such concepts as "citizenship" and "democracy", would never allow my transformation to proceed on their soil.

I had been through plenty of transformations already. There were the natural ones, of course, the sort that time and hormones grant nearly everyone, and then the transformation that comes from understanding what kind of person you really are, and finally the miracles of medicine that had allowed me to make my body fit my mind. I was lucky. In years past, the process of becoming a woman would have been clumsy and incomplete, requiring multiple surgeries, synthetic hormones, not to mention dealing with a legal system that couldn't figure out where I belonged. Now I was as fully female as anyone alive—legally, anatomically, socially, hormonally, and genetically.

And now, at the age of thirty-three, the time had come for another change. On the night of the darkest moon, on a balcony facing north and illuminated only by the stars and the flickering colors of the Aurora Borealis, they brought me a sealed, isolated computer tablet. I took it from the errand-boy and sat in the upholstered lounge chair facing out over the frigid ocean, shielded from the cold by a nearly invisible bubble of woven diamond fiber. I wore only a robe of black silk, belted loosely at my waist, but I was comfortably warm.

I could now choose precisely how my transformation would proceed. There were more options than I had expected. Immortality was a default, of course. That's what everyone wanted. Optimized strength, speed, agility and resilience were also already checked. I could have selected retractable claws, but they would have changed the appearance of my fingers too much. Likewise I didn't want fangs altering my smile. Unlike the others who arrived that day, I was not a soldier or a dictator, and did not want to be. Looking inhuman wouldn't serve my purposes. I kept it simple. I made my selections, ejected the capsule containing the nanomachines, and shut down the tablet.

I rolled back the sleeve of my robe and pressed the capsule to the wireless transceiver tattooed into my wrist. The pattern of intricate blue-green lines pulsed as they exchanged signals with the contents of the capsule. "Analyze," I said. I could feel text scrolling across the back of my hand as the AI programmed into my onskin computer started to work. I didn't need to provide details. My AI knew what I wanted.

I was buying the one thing I had always craved, but could never have—true, real dominance. I was not merely climbing another rung on the ladder of social hierarchy, but leaping from that crowded, bruising, hell-bent surge onto a completely different path. It would make all the rest irrelevant. By my very nature, I would transcend of all that. While humanity argued over who would get access to ranch-raised beef in the Canadian shield, I would dine on human blood. I lay back and watched the light show in the sky and waited.

I felt a little pinch and looked down at my hand. The AI had finished its task, and I read through the analysis summary. Everything was in order. The nanomachines had been programmed as they were supposed to be. There would be no hidden back doors into my mind, no compromise of my free will. My hosts had fulfilled their contract perfectly. With a rush of anticipation that brought a quickening to my heartbeat, I took out my personal injector, loaded the capsule, and pressed it to the thin skin inside my elbow. I felt a slight jab and shortly the anesthetic took effect. I drifted gently to sleep.

I woke to see an oriental woman leaning against the balcony rail, arms folded. The amber light of morning reflected from the clouds behind her, leaving her nearly in silhouette. Dark, straight hair fell in two narrow braids on either side of her face. She was Doctor Chiu, head of the team supervising my transformation.

"Good morning, Miss Landymore," she said. "How do you feel?" She was dressed in a white lab coat, unbuttoned to reveal a business suit beneath it. On the back of her hand, I could see the tattoos of a sophisticated onskin computer. She was not a drone; she was a member of the elite, like me.

"Well enough." I tried to sit up. My body felt about ten times heavier, and my vision swam with the effort. "A little weak," I admitted.

"That's to be expected. Your whole body has been rearranged. It takes a lot out of you. Don't worry, you'll feel much better after having something to eat." She snapped her fingers and gestured past me.

A young man stepped into my field of view—the messenger who had delivered the tablet, now stripped of the company coverall he had been wearing before. He had the clear, pale skin, blond hair and angular features of a Scandinavian. He was no doubt a local, recruited from Reykjavik or perhaps the mainland. Although he was slim, and short for a Nordic type, his frame was wrapped in well-sculpted muscle.

In the semi-darkness I caught the glint of green light from his pupils that indicated he was one of the 'augmented.' He had allowed himself to be implanted with a computer that had direct access to his brain and eyes. It was a quick route to the skills and abilities a person needed in order to be of value to the corporations, but it left him vulnerable to the influence of anyone with the skills to take control of that computer. He now lived a life of relative comfort, but he had given up a measure of his free will to get it.

Doctor Chiu gestured to me, and the man stepped closer, eyes downcast, awaiting my instructions. "I'll be nearby if you need me," said the doctor as she walked past me. I heard the doors hiss open and shut as she exited the room, leaving me with the illusion of privacy. I had no doubt that my interaction with the man would be monitored, possibly even using his own eyes as surveillance cameras, but I trusted Frjálsræði. Their business interests would not be served by divulging the secrets of their customers. Trust was an ex-nat platform's stock in trade.

"Make me ready," I said. "Pleasure me." I slid to the side of the wide chair, making room for him to sit down next to me. He leaned forward and kissed my ear, slipping one hand inside my robe to caress my breast. I was weak and sore, but his touch soothed my skin, and his short blond hair smelled of sage and rosemary. A chuckle rose to my throat as I thought of a slice of rare roast beef crusted with herbs.

My body responded to his touch, warming as his lips brushed my neck and shoulder, shuddering as his hand lightly squeezed my nipple and then moved lower, across my ribs and abdomen, and then down into the curls between my legs. His fingers did not hesitate when they found three hard nubs at the apex of my sex rather than one, but he would have known what to expect. Wet noises came from the place where his fingers met my body, punctuating my soft moans. I wanted to take charge, to flip places with him, throw him to the floor and ride him, but I was still too weak. "I hunger," I said, and he nodded.

With tender grace he touched the control to flatten the chair, then spread my legs to hang over either side. He was erect already, his slim uncircumcised cock no doubt under his conscious control. This was one of the many gifts for which he had traded ownership of his mind. There was no great sense of fullness as he slipped it inside me, but I could feel new muscles stimulated by the presence of his organ, new neural pathways activated, new reflexes engaged. His cock felt better inside me than any had ever felt before. My vagina had been promoted to the general manager of the erogenous zone department, headquartered in those two muscular knots on either side of my clit.

As the man's thighs tensed with his thrusts, I slipped my hand down between our bodies to explore my new anatomy. My clit was just as sensitive as it had always been, but it felt very good to massage the lumps under the skin, now swollen to the size of grapes, that flanked it. Pressed from within by his cock, squeezed from without by my fingers, they jostled against my clit, multiplying my pleasure. It was purest ecstasy.

I had never been driven so quickly toward orgasm. I was on the fast track, stopping at the usual stages of arousal and plateau only long enough to acknowledge that I had been there, check off the box, and move on. As the tension in my body grew tighter, the knots bore down as well, elongating, drawing in. Climax arched my back, clenched my thighs, and triggered the culmination of my new body.

Two bone-hard needles shot out of the new organs in my pussy, piercing the man's cock at the base, hooking into him and holding him there while they delivered their potent venom. He tensed as it took hold, and then shouted in pain and pleasure, climaxing spontaneously, growling and clawing, face contorted, body twisting, cock swelling and pulsing inside me.

A satisfying warmth filled my pussy, then my abdomen, and the weakness I had felt dissipated like fog in the morning sun. I retracted my fangs and pushed the man back. He fell away, cock still hard, blood still dribbling weakly from the tip. As I rose, he collapsed onto the bed, still alive but drained.

Near the door, a basin of water steamed next to a small stack of towels. I retrieved my robe and pulled it over my shoulders, then soaked the washcloth and bathed my cunt. In spite of the tremendous amount of blood the man had ejaculated, there was very little on the exterior of my body. Almost all of it had been absorbed.

I pressed the button on the intercom next to the door. "All finished," I said.

"Was everything to your satisfaction, ma'am?"

"Yes. Perfectly."

* * * *

I returned to the everyday world of the headquarters of Global and Orbital Holdings, LLC with a completely new outlook. My colleagues on the Water Planning Board noticed when I pointed out that while our choices for the integrity checks on the AI running the Sicilian desalinization plant might not leave us vulnerable to a lawsuit, an accident there might very well have a negative effect on the project bottom line in the long run.

I stood up at the table, and instructed my onskin AI to transmit my figures to the display hologram in the middle of the room. "Having a virtual monopoly on fresh water is indeed a very profitable position to be in, but if the supply were interrupted for even a few days, the number of customers would likely be drastically reduced."

My simulations and projections were not materially different than what I had presented before, but things had changed. I had changed. Before their onskin AI's had finished chattering to each other over the office network, they had agreed to strengthen the protocols, seeing the expense as a modest investment compared to the potential risk. The committee chair nodded to me, and I sat down again, confident that the whole room now saw me in a different light.

I kept myself well-fed. Before my trip to the ex-nat platform I had lined up a whole herd of augmented middle-managers and experts, people whose brain implants answered to me and my onskin AI rather than their ostensible owners. They would believe what I told them to believe, remember what I wanted them to remember, and do what I ordered them to do. There were enough of them that I could visit each one only once a month, take my fill, and leave them enough time to recover until I returned. I made sure that their grocery deliveries included plenty of beef from the new ranches on the Canadian shield.

They would need plenty of iron and protein in their diets.

It wasn't long before my boss, Vice President of Critical Resources, invited me to lunch on her private airship. All around our table, windows provided a view of the city in all its bustling splendor, on a level with the highest of the corporate arcologies. Shimmering holographic billboards advertised the latest in hyper-luxury goods, invisible to the groundlings below who would never be able to afford them. I paid the signs little heed.

Scoring this invitation was a very good sign. A lunch invitation with Victoria LaPlace meant that I was on the fast track, that I was being considered for a promotion. I might even be invited to her bed. That would be an even better sign. Under my black, knee-length dress I wore my programmable nanofabric underwear. There wasn't anything more convenient than that for someone preparing for a possible liaison.

Miss LaPlace did not look like a formidable woman. She was petite, with features that had the slightest hint of childlike innocence—large eyes, turned-up nose, and pale patches on her cheekbones that set them off nicely against her dark skin. She kept her dark dreadlocks in a ponytail bundle down her back, and wore a sleeveless royal blue vested suit that showed off the golden tracery of the onskin computer covering most of her left arm.

We dined on fresh meteorfish, a brand new variety engineered to be resistant to radiation and tolerant of zero-gravity, from the first catch to be brought down from orbit. It was seasoned with salt specifically harvested at the Baffin Island desalinization plant, and exotic spices grown in the newest Kamchatka plantations. The roasted peppers came from the greenhouses of Finland, and the rice in the reclaimed Potomac wetlands. The silverware was made from metal mined in our asteroids, and the china had been fired in kilns powered by our satellites. It was a meal that represented everything Global and Orbital had accomplished.

"Nothing from Antarctica?" I asked, once I recognized the theme for the afternoon.

"The wood of the furniture," said Miss LaPlace. "Manufactured at McMurdo Township."

"Ah, of course. You caught me on that one."

"Nonsense. It would have been gauche to turn the chair over to find the maker's mark."

The conversation continued in a similar vein, little more than small talk, until the dishes were cleared and she sent her servant to fetch cognac and cigars. I wasn't sated, really, having only nibbled at most of the food, but I would be fine once I got back to the ground and visited one of my devoted donors.

"I've actually never smoked a cigar before," I said. "I've only used the electronic cigarettes. Cancer risk, and all that."

"Ah, but you don't have to worry about that anymore, do you?" she asked, as she clipped the end from her cigar and slid the box toward me.

I gave her an innocent look and imitated her action. "How do you mean?"

"You thought your trip to Frjálsræði was a secret?" She pronounced the difficult Icelandic name perfectly.

178

"Come now, dear. You know I keep tabs on all of my most promising executives." She lit her cigar, puffed out fragrant smoke, and then rose to bring the lighter over to me.

The graceful thing to do was to acknowledge her superiority in this arena. I nodded to her and allowed her to light my cigar. The cigar was sweet and aromatic, filling my senses without overpowering them. I could practically taste the wisps of blue smoke with my eyes. I didn't mind her display of dominance in the slightest. It didn't matter. I was the ultimate carnivore, top of the food chain. I fed on human blood. I could afford to be magnanimous with petty social conventions like these. "I hope you don't mind the indulgence," I said.

"Not at all." She poured two glasses of cognac from a crystal decanter, still standing in front of me. The liquid was the same dark amber color as the skin on the back of her hand. "It would be rather hypocritical of me, wouldn't you say?"

"You've been there as well?" I asked, taking a sip of cognac that fit with the cigar like the keystone of an arch, its flavor blending perfectly with that of the smoke.

She nodded. "In fact, I'd like to propose a childish little game, if you'll permit the impropriety."

I raised an eyebrow, leaning back in my chair to show how nonchalant I could be about such things. "What did you have in mind?"

"You show me yours, and I'll show you mine."

I smiled a wicked grin. "Sounds like fun."

"You first," she said, after a puff on her cigar.

"Alright." I stood up, pushed the cigar box and my cognac away from the table, and pulled my dress up over my head, staring into Miss LaPlace's dark eyes. She took in my figure and pursed her lips briefly at the sight. The nanomachines in my blood maintained my figure along with everything else, giving me exactly the shape I wanted without my having to worry about pesky things like diet or exercise. My breasts were a modest size, not big enough to lead anyone to believe I was trying to sell myself on sex alone but not too small, either, and my waist-to-hip ratio was in perfect proportion. A voluptuous body was the marker of a drone, someone whose form was sculpted to please others, not oneself. Elites were slim and lean, with the clean shape of a predator. I could tell by the smile playing on Miss LaPlace's eyes that she approved.

I ran my fingers down the control strips on the straps of my bra. The nanomachines that made up the fabric of the cups reconfigured themselves in response, rolling down to the underside, leaving only the structural supports on either side. Instead of covering my breasts, the open triangles accentuated the fact that they were exposed, framing them with dark ribbons. When I touched the control strip on my panties, they changed similarly, revealing my carefully trimmed pubic hair. The curly patch of fur was under control, kept away from my labia and measured in extent, but left to grow as long as it cared to. It was a fashion statement of its own, a declaration of my intention to live life on my own terms.

I sat on the table, spread my thighs, and leaned back onto my elbows. "There you are."

Miss LaPlace stood over me for a moment, looking me over, evaluating me. She reached out and flicked a nipple with one long fingernail, sending a spark through my chest. "Part of the package?" she asked.

"Well, they're mostly the same as before. A bit more sensitive."

"Of course. Isn't it nice?" She pinched one nipple between her fingers and then stroked that hand down along my flank. I felt the hair on the back of my neck stand up, and I arched my back, half displaying for her and half out of honest pleasure.

As her hand reached my hip, she brought my chair close and sat down. Her fingers traced the thick ribbons on either side of my pussy appreciatively before exploring my dangerously engineered flesh, rubbing the little knots where I kept my fangs, running her fingers down over my sex, and leaning in to inhale deeply while smiling up at me. "They did a good job," she said.

I sighed in pleasure and satisfaction. "Indeed. You can't believe how good that feels."

"Oh, I can," she said.

"So are you going to show me?"

"In a bit." She leaned in a little closer, and took a tentative lick between the two nodules, spreading them apart to take a direct swipe at my clit. Then, with gradually more maddening results, she licked and bit and nuzzled every other part of my cunt except those three little knots of flesh. When I tried to encourage her to go back there, she deflected my hands, or pushed my butt back down on the table, forcing the tease to deeper and deeper frustration. She was strong, as strong as I was, and had the advantage of position. "Not yet," she said. "You're not ready."

"God!" I finally shouted. "I'm dying here! Make me come already." I knew she wanted it. I could have smelled her musky arousal from across the room.

She stood up, pressing her firm belly against my sex, and licked one nipple. "I think you've forgotten who is the boss here."

"Please," I whimpered. "You're driving me insane."

She cupped my pussy in one hand and squeezed the outer lips together between her fingers. "You want it?" she asked.

I nodded, desperately.

"You're sure?"

"Please!"

"Good." With that she stood up, pulled up the hem of her skirt, and thrust a thick, hard *something* inside me.

"Is that... ?" I managed to say, past the surprise and pleasure. If it was a strap-on, it was the most realistic I had ever felt.

"It's my cock." She thrust hard against me, her hands under my thighs, holding my hips at an angle that made it hit firmly on the upper wall of my vagina.

My head spun. She was offering herself for me to feed on, she had to be, but in the most dominant, controlling way I could imagine. Would I be punished if I bit her? Was she expecting me to control myself? It didn't matter—I was too confused to do anything but let the feelings slide through me as her member ebbed and surged inside me. Each inward push ground her body against mine, squeezing my fang-roots against my pubic bone and investing my arousal afresh. There was no holding back, no resisting.

I felt my fangs plunge into Miss LaPlace's cock, felt them sink deep, felt them pump their neurotoxin, as ecstasy tore into me. I slammed my fists against the table and the wood cracked. I shrieked so loud I thought my eardrums would burst.

A moment later, the poison took effect, and I felt my body fill with hot, thick chief-operating-officer blood. Her nails dug into my thighs, penetrating deeply into my skin, and I felt thin streams of blood run down toward my crotch. The pain of the wounds blended with my pleasure, laying me flat against the table. I thought for a moment that I would lose consciousness. My fangs retracted, and I heard a thump as Miss LaPlace fell back into the chair.

My senses swam. My body alternated hot and cold, and when I tried to move, I only twitched. My thoughts wouldn't string together. It was like having a fever, but that was impossible; I would never get sick again. I lay there, panting, unable to recover, for what seemed like hours.

When the symptoms cleared enough for me to sit up, I saw her calmly licking her hands clean, bloody clothes covering whatever organ it was she had used on me. A strange glow formed around her face like a halo. Her scent, still heavy in the air along with the smell of blood and spilled cognac, was ambrosia. I wanted more of it, I needed it, and I found myself sliding from the table to kneel at her feet. I was dizzy with lust, paralyzed with adoration. "Mistress" was the only word I could speak.

She smiled down at me, her smile broader and more sincere than I'd ever seen before. It was pure delight, and seeing it should have made me feel afraid. It was the smile of someone who had *won*.

And I felt the deepest, most profound pleasure that I had pleased her. "Mistress," I said again.

She reached down and stroked my hair. I could smell her sweet saliva clinging to her skin, and it turned me on. Some corner of my mind that was still under my own control understood what must have happened. She too had visited the blood engineers of Frjálsræði.

Only she hadn't ordered from the menu. She had a special request. She had purchased a nanotech system for her own body that would be carried along with the blood, linking with the nanotech system of any vampire that fed on her. I was as much a slave to it now as my drones were to their implant computers.

My free will was gone forever, and I didn't care. It was a small price to pay, for such bliss.

* * * *

Vampires, Limited
© Lisabet Sarai

"Next!' Lara stabbed the intercom button with a crimson-tipped finger. She tilted her chair back and closed her eyes, trying to summon some enthusiasm for the next sacrificial lamb. Who would have thought it would be so difficult? With the current craze for all things vampiric, finding a new model or two with the appropriate pallor and unearthly allure should have been a piece of cake. The city teemed with Dracula wannabes. Why were the ones who showed up at her office so lame?

She needed new faces, new excitement. The poster-sized cover images on her walls featured the dark-haired, chalk-faced, chisel-chinned hunks that her readers expected. Swathed in black, poised above the vulnerable flesh of their gorgeous prey with fangs bared, they reeked of danger and desire. An occasional female vamp joined them, jet curls tumbling into her pale cleavage, carmine lips shining as though already painted with blood.

The images were sexy, edgy, and irresistibly hip. In its first year, *Vamp* magazine had broken the circulation record for a new publication. It had become the de facto authority for the burgeoning vampire subculture. It covered the fashions, the clubs, the bands, the latest pseudo-vampiric celebrities. In the back, advertisements for skin bleaching cosmetics and fang implants mingled with the personal ads. "Attractive SWF seeks dominant SWM for blood-sucking adventures".

The cultural wave was far from cresting, but Lara knew that she had to keep innovating, or she'd be left in the dust by her copycat competitors.

A knock brought her back to the here and now. "Come in," she called, trying to erase the impatience from her voice. She flicked her black bangs out of her eyes and assumed what she hoped was a welcoming expression.

A man glided in through the door, and Lara thought for an instant that there had been a mild earthquake. Reality somehow shifted. Her stomach dropped away, as though her roller coaster car had just reached a peak and plunged down the other side. The office and its somber furnishings suddenly looked more solid, hyper-real, every detail visible.

With some difficulty, Lara focused on the blond young man standing in front of her desk. "Good afternoon." Reflexively she took the portfolio that he handed her. "I'm Lara Carter, publisher of *Vamp*."

"Jim," her visitor answered in a broad American accent. "Jim Henderson. Thank you for taking the time to see me, Ms. Carter."

Jim Henderson was attractive, no question of that, but Lara could see immediately that he was all wrong. He was slender rather than muscular, though he moved well as he seated himself across from her. His straw-colored curls and ruddy complexion fairly screamed health and youth. She'd never seen anyone who looked less undead. He had such an open, intelligent face that Lara couldn't imagine him looking crafty or menacing. He wasn't even wearing black. His tan slacks and robin's-egg sport shirt highlighted his trim physique and heightened the blue of his eyes, but no vampire (at least, no London vampire) would ever be caught wearing such a costume.

"You think that I'm the wrong type for your vampire mag." It was a statement, not a question, and mirrored her thoughts so accurately that Lara was startled.

"Well, you certainly don't fit the stereotype. You're a bit too —um—wholesome for our readers."

Jim's laugh held an odd, bitter edge. "Take a look at my photos before you make a decision, Ms. Carter."

Lara flipped open the portfolio and leafed through the contents. There was no resume. The first two pictures were head shots, clearly professional, and Lara had to admit that the man's smoldering gaze was dark and seductive enough to send a chill up her spine, despite the blue eyes and fair coloring.

"Do you have any experience?"

"Depends what you mean. But modeling experience— no. I've never been a model."

"Why do you want to work for *Vamp*, then? What did you do before?"

"I was in college." He didn't seem to want to say anymore about his past. "When I saw your ad, it seemed natural to apply."

Lara appraised him with the hard-headedness that was her trademark. He was quite gorgeous. She wouldn't mind taking him home. However, she didn't need a dilettante, a college kid on a lark. At the moment, *Vamp* was her life's work. She'd quit a good job at *Vogue* to follow her hunch and it had paid off. She needed models who were as serious as she was.

"I'm not a dilettante. I am serious about this job." Lara's eyes narrowed. His sensitivity was certainly unnerving. "Take a look at the next few photographs. Please."

She flipped to the next picture and sucked in her breath. The image was incredible. The scene was familiar but the intensity made it new. She scarcely recognized Jim. He wore a black velvet cape with a red satin lining and white gloves. His face was poised above an exquisite girl with long red hair that barely hid her obviously naked body. His full lips curled into a snarl, displaying the most realistic fangs that Lara had ever seen. Blood dripped from those fangs, pooling in shiny droplets on the woman's creamy skin. Blood welled from the puncture wounds clearly visible on her neck. The man's eyes were not on his prey, who wore a look of languid ecstasy. They were focused toward the viewer, burning with a palpable hunger that made Lara swallow hard.

'Wow," she whispered. The photo had a dramatic, visceral effect. Her heart raced. Her palms became sweaty. Underneath her black jersey, she felt her nipples tighten into aching knots. "That's amazing. How did you manage it?"

"Try the next picture." The man's body was tense, as though he was working hard to hold something back. Slowly, tearing herself away from the soulful gaze in the photo, she turned it over.

The photograph that followed ripped her apart. Although vampiric in theme, it was nothing like the camp pictures that her publication featured. The same red-haired woman lay nude on a satin-draped bier, graceful and pale. Her wrists crossed on her abdomen, just below the modest swell of her perfect breasts. Her face was turned toward the camera, her eyes closed, her lips parted. A trail of crimson fluid trickled from her neck, across the white satin and onto the stone floor.

Behind the bier stood the vampire. His right hand held a white candle that fitfully illuminated the arches of the vault. His left cupped his victim's breast, thumb resting lightly on her prominent nipple.

His blond hair was pushed back from his brow, damp with sweat. His skin was flushed with the blood that he had swallowed, the blood that still smeared his lips. Looking into those eyes, eyes dark as hell, Lara felt it all: his grief, his guilt and his awful, all-consuming lust.

Who was she, the ethereal, terribly convincing victim? And who, who was he?

She didn't see him move. Yet all at once he was behind her, his hands on her shoulders, murmuring in her ear. "Barbara was her name. She was my girlfriend, back in college. A terrible mistake."

He was so close, she should have felt the heat of his body, but it was as if a mannequin was pressed against her, instead of a living person. She could smell him, though, a sharp grassy scent that made her think of the country and wide open spaces.

Casually he trailed a finger up the side of her neck and circled her earlobe. A shiver raced through her, winding tight around her nipples, spiraling down to her sex. He nipped at her ear, playful, but hard enough to make her gasp. "As for me, you know who I am, don't you? Or at least, what I am."

Lara knew what he was saying. She just couldn't accept it.

"Here." Still behind her, he grabbed her hand and placed her fingers on his throat. His skin was cooler than the air, cool and smooth as marble. "Do you feel any pulse?"

"No—but—it's just not possible. It's just a myth. A fashion, a fad. Everyone these days pretends..."

He brought her wrist to his lips, flicking his tongue over the spot where the veins were closest to the surface. His mouth was hot, unlike the rest of him. A violent shudder of desire rocked her body. "Close your eyes," he murmured.

I should call off this farce now, Lara thought, but she obeyed anyway. Something pricked at her flesh where he held it against his mouth, the tiniest sting, hardly deserving the name pain. Then there was heat, and a pulling, not at her wrist but somehow at her heart, which leaped up in response and began to pump at twice its normal rate.

Red flooded the space behind her eyelids, scarlet, crimson, three-dimensional eddies of color like billowing clouds. A brief icicle of fear stabbed at her, then melted as warm, sweet pleasure flowed through her limbs. Her nipples, her pussy, everywhere there was this hot, wet current, aching and yet somehow not urgent.

"Relax," he whispered. "Let go." She heard his voice, coming from a long way off. She saw his eyes, burning through the red haze. They had darkened from blue to empty black. She felt herself tumbling into their depths. Some last fragment of self-consciousness cried out for her to resist, but she ignored it. He was too strong, his will irresistible, the gifts he offered too precious to refuse. She let herself drift. He cradled then released her. She felt herself beginning to drown in the scarlet river of his blood lust.

The shock of separation drove black spikes of pain into her temples. She opened her eyes, gasping for breath. Motes of red swam in her vision. She twisted around to look at him, in wonder and terror.

"Sorry," he shrugged. "I didn't know how else to convince you."

"You're—you're the real thing, aren't you?" Lara thought her chest would burst. "Nosferatu. Undead." She rubbed at her throbbing head. "I never believed..."

"Believe," he said, his voice low and solemn. Then all at once was back in his chair, leaving her heart slamming against her ribs. He smiled at her, that wide open, American country-boy smile. Lara worked to catch her breath, to calm herself to some semblance of normalcy.

It wasn't possible. Vampires were a fiction, a legend. They were creatures of fantasy and nightmare. For some reason, the notion of vampires tapped into something fundamental in the human imagination. She knew dozens, maybe hundreds, of people who desperately wanted vampires to be real. These people were the engine of her success. However, even the most obsessed, the ones who caught and ate flies and slept in coffins in the cellar, knew the truth.

And now, here, that truth was being challenged.

He read her doubts, in her mind or on her face. He disappeared suddenly, then reappeared at her side with a glass of water. "Looks like you could use this." Another blink and he was back where he started, smiling at her across the desk. The water was there, at her elbow, proof that she hadn't been hallucinating. She took a sip and stopped fighting the evidence of her senses. It wasn't possible that he was a vampire. But it was true.

"Are you very ancient?" she asked, finally. The question sounded absurd. What was she doing, continuing the interview? Jim laughed, wholeheartedly this time.

"I'm twenty four. Or I was, that night five years ago at the frat party, when somebody's girlfriend's sister turned me. I admit that I was drunk. Barbara had just told me that she wanted a commitment, and I knew I wasn't ready. I told her I loved her, but that wasn't enough. So I went off, got plastered, and the next thing I knew I was in bed with this slutty-looking brunette who had very sharp teeth." Lara couldn't help giggling. His tale was such a contrast to the mythology that she marketed.

"And then? What happened next? What about Barbara?"

Jim's face grew shadowed. "Look, I don't really want to talk about it. Not now, not here. Can we go somewhere quiet and dark for a drink?"

"You can drink? I mean, besides—well, you know."

"Sure. I can't eat solid food, though. It's awful, because my senses are unnaturally acute. I can smell a juicy steak grilling half a block away. Pure torture." He sighed. "Anyway, what about the job? Do you still think that I'm unqualified, Ms. Carter?"

Lara took note of the challenge in his voice. Her body

still trembled at the proximity of an honest-to-goodness creature of the night, but her mind was working overtime. How could she best use him to further her goals? To expand her vampire-themed empire? His photos were far too raw for her audience. Could he project the same level of intensity in a less extreme scene? And what about his co-models? Could he elicit the same sort of rapturous response from them that she had seen in Barbara's face? Without actually taking them, of course?

She imagined herself in the woman's position, offering her throat to those vicious fangs. The notion was seductive. She had just been given a taste. To give in completely to that kind of power—to be overwhelmed, consumed by an unnatural hunger —the temptation was almost overwhelming. She'd always wanted the power, never considered letting go. Now the thought of offering herself to this creature made her damp with desire. A wave of dizziness swept over her, followed by a surge of fear.

"Don't worry." Jim interrupted her lurid imaginings. "Seriously, I know how to control myself. Every few weeks I raid a hospital or Red Cross blood bank, then fix up the computerized records so the inventory won't be missed. I'm only dangerous when I really hungry."

"And I don't mind if you want to use me to build your business. That's why I'm here."

Lara blushed. It was difficult to remember that this apparently naive young man could read her thoughts. Did he know that her knickers were wet? His good-natured grin told her that he did.

She stood, working to regain her composure, and held out her hand. "Well, Jim. I'm pleased to welcome you to Vampires, Limited. Shall we go for that drink?"

"Sure." He helped settle her cape around her shoulders, then held the door for her. *An old fashioned gentleman*, Lara thought. *How charming*. She pictured a shoot, Jim at the door of a crypt, politely ushering some juicy young thing into its depths. It might work. Then she noticed him watching her, a half-smile on his ripe lips. *Damn*. She couldn't get used to being so transparent.

Her assistant Felicia raised a carefully penciled eyebrow when they emerged into the anteroom. Like everyone who worked for *Vamp*, Felicia wore black clothes and white makeup. "Are you leaving, Ms. Carter? There are still two candidates waiting to see you."

"Tell them to come back tomorrow, please. I'm going out with Mr. Henderson to discuss business."

They walked in silence through the chilly, overcast afternoon, headed for one of Lara's favorite pubs. The pavement was crowded. Businessmen and shoppers bustled by, not giving Jim and Lara a second glance. It would be dusk soon, and rush hour would be begin in earnest.

Lara stopped short, staring at Jim's figure, bundled up in his overcoat. "It's daytime," she accused, stabbing her finger into his chest.

"So?"

"Well, what about the sun? I thought that vampires couldn't be about during the day?"

"Not much sun," Jim commented, peering up at the leaden sky. "That's one reason I came to England, actually. I can't handle direct sunlight, but in weather like this, I'm fine. Sunscreen or a hat helps, too."

"But—then you're not really a creature of the night!"

Jim grabbed the hand poking him. Slowly and deliberately, he rubbed his thumb over the tiny puncture wound on her wrist. Lara trembled, remembering. "Sort of depends on your definition, doesn't it?" His smile made her cringe with embarrassed desire. When he released her, she struggled not to sink to her knees. He took her arm and led her in the direction of the pub.

"Don't believe everything you hear. Garlic doesn't bother me. I could sleep in a church or take a bath in holy water with no ill effects. Electromagnetic radiation, on the other hand, could probably kill me. Even a cell phone makes me weak. A taser would likely do me in."

Lara shifted the bag with her phone to her other arm.

"Loud noises are a problem, because my hearing is so sensitive. Explosions. Sirens. I went deaf for a week, early on, when my roommate turned up the volume on Ozzy Osbourne. Now I always carry earplugs."

"What about flying? Or becoming invisible?" Lara remembered the way he seemed to appear and disappear in her office.

"I can move extremely fast, when I want to. However, I have nothing whatsoever to do with bats!"

They arrived at Donnie's, the place she'd been aiming for. It was, as he had requested, dark and quiet, especially at four in the afternoon. Settling them in a booth at the back, Lara ordered a gin and tonic. Jim asked for a glass of cabernet, grinning at her raised eyebrows.

They shucked off their outerwear. Jim sat next to her on the bench. His thigh was a mere inch from hers. It was just so strange that she couldn't feel his body heat through her tights. She wondered, suddenly, what his cock was like. Would it be cool like his neck, or warm like his lips?

"I'd be happy to show you," Jim laughed. Lara felt the flush climbing to the roots of her hair.

"Damn it, can you hear every bloody thing that I'm thinking?"

"Not really. Sometimes it's all muddled together. But it seems as though the more emotion there is associated with a thought, the more clearly it comes through."

Gently, he reached over and brushed her bangs away

from her eyes. "You seem to be quite an emotional person, Lara."

Emotional? That certainly conflicted with her self-image. She saw herself as rational, businesslike, ambitious. She didn't let her feelings intrude on her life or influence important decisions. Her two ex-boyfriends had both called her "cold", but never mind. She was simply disciplined. Self-controlled.

It was difficult to maintain control, though, sitting next to this beautiful and seductive—phenomenon.

"So—why did you answer my ad, really? What were you looking for? With your powers, surely you can get all the money you might want."

"I was lonely. Even though I don't look much like Dracula, people sense something. They don't necessarily recognize what I am, but they know, instinctively, that I'm not one of them. Unless I use my abilities to charm then, they shun me."

Lara nodded, recalling her odd sensations when he had entered her office.

"I thought that, working for a vampire magazine, I'd be surrounded by people who were used to the idea of the undead. Who found it glamorous and sexy. Maybe they'd react differently from ordinary people. But now I don't know." A shadow crossed Jim's face. "It might be too dangerous for me to be working for you."

"Dangerous for you? Or for me?"

"Possibly both." He sipped his wine. It stained his full lips purple. Lara briefly imagined kissing him, then struggled to suppress the thought before he could catch it. Lost in his own concerns, he didn't react. Lara fidgeted with the lime in her drink.

"Tell me about Barbara," she asked finally. "The woman in the photos." As soon as she saw his ravaged face, she was sorry for the question.

"I was stupid, inexperienced. And we were so much in love. When I realized what I had become, I crawled to her on my hands and knees and begged her forgiveness. I was so terribly sorry to have ruined our plans for a life together. Barbara, though, had other ideas. She pointed out that, according to all information, we could now share eternity. All I had to do was turn her, make her into a vampire too.

"I was reluctant, but she convinced me. She was so beautiful, I couldn't bear the notion that she would eventually age and die while I'd live forever.

"We planned the ritual carefully, almost as if it were our wedding ceremony..."

"The photos–" Lara interrupted.

"Right." Jim laughed bitterly. "I set up the camera to record it all. The initiation of my beloved into the realm of the undead. But it all went terribly wrong." He choked back a sob. Lara felt a sympathetic lump in her throat.

"What happened?"

"Everybody knows how you make a new vampire. First you drain the victim's blood, bringing her close to death. Then you allow her to drink your blood. That's what we planned. That's what we did. It was incredible, terrifying and ecstatic."

"But?"

"But she died. I couldn't save her. I couldn't turn her. Since then I've learned the truth."

Lara was silent, waiting.

"To create a new vampire, you must suck the victim's blood while you're physically connected. While you're having sex."

"You're joking!"

"No, it's no joke. That's why I ended up this way. That girl at the party—all she really wanted was my blood. But one thing led to another, and eventually we were fucking.

I don't think she really understood either."

No wonder his little demonstration had produced such an intense effect. For him, blood lust and sexual desire were inextricably entwined. The instinctive drive to reproduce, to bring more souls over the boundary of death into the shadowy world that he inhabited, this was something he could not deny, and could only imperfectly control.

Lara knew she should be frightened. She should get out his seductive presence before she made a final, incorrigible mistake. The risk, the pure reality of it, only made her want him more.

He was watching her. She could feel his eyes on her lips, on her throat, on the rise and fall of her breasts as her breath quickened.

She glanced around the bar, filling up now that it was after five. Donnie's was not known as a "blood" bar, but still, she noticed half a dozen men wearing capes and pale make up, plus two or three women in slinky black dresses and wigs. It was pathetic, the way they all craved a fleeting taste of inhuman power, a brush with immortality. And here she sat, thigh to thigh with the genuine article.

"I don't fully understand it," Jim said, obviously catching her thoughts once again. "Why would they want to be me? Power's nice, but overall, I live a pretty lonely and miserable existence."

"Maybe—maybe I can make you feel less lonely. For a little while." Lara cradled his cheek for an instant, then pulled his mouth to hers. His lips were soft as any flesh, warm and muscular as they met and molded to her own lips. She tasted the wine he had been drinking, with background flavors of iron and salt. His tongue, too, felt human, jousting against hers, exploring, questioning.

Her rigid nipples pressed rudely through the stretchy

fabric of her top, pleading for his attention. Of course he knew what she wanted. Without breaking the kiss, he cupped both breasts, tracing symmetrical circles around the tips. Her pussy clenched. Her thighs opened involuntarily. She rocked back and forth on the bench, rubbing her clit against the hard wood.

"Please," she moaned against his open mouth, and then was silent, realizing that she did not have to say anything. He broke the kiss to throw a twenty pound note on the table, then pulled her to his chest.

"Imagine your apartment," he said, close to her ear. "Think about your bedroom. And hold on tight."

She took a breath and was swallowed by sudden, utter darkness. She could feel the bulk of Jim's body pressed against hers, but she could see nothing. A howling wind tore at her clothes. Her ears rang with the clang of a hundred untuned bells. Fear rose in her throat, but before she could scream, it was over.

Light returned. She stood on the shag carpet in her room clutching at Jim's shirt. Her knees buckled. He held her up, held her against him.

"I—what—how—?" she babbled.

"Hush. There's no need for talk now." He bent to kiss her again, and this time she felt the fire stirring deep within him. She sensed his unnatural strength as he lifted her onto the bed and knelt between her legs. He peeled off her tights and drew down her soaked knickers without comment. She felt the air stir as he bent his mouth close to her yearning pussy, but no breath. Her clit beat like a tiny heart, swollen with blood. She knew that he could smell the blood through her skin, that for him it overwhelmed the tidal scent of her sex.

Take me. Before the idea was fully formed, his tongue was gliding through her slit, slithering among her folds, lapping at her juices as if they were in fact the fluid that he most craved. She arched and twisted under him, opening herself to him body and mind. He stabbed his tongue into her depths, then pulled back to suck hard on the aching bead of flesh at the apex. Sensation rippled out from that center to all her extremities.

She pinched her nipples through her top, shuddering as the pleasure looped back to her pussy where he stroked it to a higher pitch. He sucked vigorously, holding her lower lips apart so that he could penetrate more deeply, smoothing her soaked curls with his thumbs. Lara writhed against him, burying his face in her wet depths. He didn't need to breathe, she realized. He could go on like this forever.

It might have been that thought that pushed her over. It might have been the sudden pain of his teeth nipping her clit, or the invasion of a slippery finger into her rear hole. Whatever the ultimate stimulus, her climax seized and ripped through her. Ecstasy surged and then crested. She raced screaming and shuddering down the other side, spasms of pleasure shaking her until she was limp as a rag doll.

"I want you naked," Jim said, his voice soft but full of command. "I want to be able to see your pulse. I want to feel the heat of the blood in your veins." He lifted her to her feet, and she let him, still dazed and weak from her orgasm. He eased the jersey over her head, baring her small, freckled breasts and taut, wine-dark nipples. He reached around back to unzip her, giving her bottom a squeeze on the way, and guided her pencil skirt over her hips to the floor.

Lara let him undress her, passively enjoying his touch. She couldn't comprehend the lassitude that overwhelmed her. Normally she was the aggressor in the bedroom. Now all she wanted was to lie back and let him do whatever pleased him.

He arranged her on the champagne satin coverlet. The smooth, cool fabric caressed her bottom and back. He crouched between her spread thighs, naked now himself. His cock was huge and pale with a livid purple head. *Hot or cool?* she wondered again. He half-smiled in response, and buried his undead flesh inside her.

Cold, deathly cold, and hard as granite, he filled her, stretched her to the point of pain. Panic rose in her, fueled by the weird sensations that his inhuman cock wakened. Surely he'd tear her apart. People always talked about cocks as if they were steel or stone, but this was no metaphor. Icy fingers crept through her depths, making her shiver violently.

Concern filled Jim's handsome face. "Should I stop? Is it too much?" At the sound of his voice, something changed. The diamond-hard rod embedded in her flesh grew warm, melting her resistance and her fear. The pleasure began to flow again, rich and sweet as honey. Full as she was, she wanted to be fuller. His cock owned her now, and that was what she wanted. She wanted him to take her, to use her, to consume her.

He heard. He pulled his cock halfway out of her clinging flesh, then rammed it back in, wringing a whimper of pain from her. *More,* she thought. He pierced her once again, slowly, letting her feel the length and breadth of him taking control. Lara gasped. His smooth, immutable flesh swept over her aching clit, waking shimmering echoes of her climax.

She gazed up at him and saw his eyes growing dark. His lips were parted. Peeking out she glimpsed the sharp tips of his fangs. A thrill raced through her. This was not fantasy. This was real.

More. He started to fuck her in earnest, thrusting hard and fast. She gripped the coverlet and arched up to him, still wanting more. The force of his strokes shook her whole body. Without effort, without expectation, she came, screaming and thrashing beneath him. Still he drove his cock into her again and again, until he had wrung a third climax from her ravaged body.

He hovered over her, supporting his weight with his arms while his pelvis jerked, his cock drilling her pussy with metronomic regularity. His face was beautiful and terrible. His eyes were black pools of lust. His lips were drawn into a tense grimace, fully baring his fangs. His nostrils flared. Lara knew that he was scenting her blood.

It seemed now that she could read *his* thoughts. She sensed his desperate hunger and his fight to control it. He wanted her, wanted her body, in a way that no man ever would. The force of his need stunned her. She remembered the images he had brought to her office, with new understanding. Being a vampire was not about power or immortality. It was about unending, insatiable lust.

Pity and desire welled up simultaneously. Nothing else mattered but this awful hunger, which only she could satisfy. She turned her head to the side, exposing the pulsing artery in her neck. "Take me," she moaned to him, in between thrusts. "Taste me. Drink me. Make me yours."

"No," he forced out the words between gritted teeth. "I can't. I won't." His thrusts slowed, though his cock remained embedded in her pussy.

Lara tightened her inner muscles. His flesh jerked inside her. "You need me."

"It's not right."

Lara reached down to where they were joined and dabbled her fingers for a moment, gathering her juices. Then she trailed her sticky fingers down from her ear to her collarbone, across her pulse, smearing the secretions across her blood-heated flesh. The smell of ripe pussy rose around her. "Just a taste," she cajoled. "You know that you want to. You don't have to take me all the way."

"I won't be able to stop."

"I'll stop you."

Jim laughed bitterly. "Oh, no you won't. Don't you remember my little demonstration? Would you have been able to stop me then?"

A tiny needle of fear pricked at Lara's heart. She ignored it. She wanted this, and he would die without it. She knew that she could maintain control.

"Please?"

"No!"

Lara couldn't bear the anguish in his voice. She raised her wrist to her mouth, the one he had punctured earlier, and tore off the scab with her teeth. A crimson droplet welled from the spot. She forced it to his lips. "Drink!"

With a strangled groan, the vampire seized her hand. He used his fangs to open the wound further. Pain flowed from her sliced wrist to her soaked pussy, where it inexplicably morphed into pleasure. She felt his suction pulling at her life blood, felt her heart laboring to adjust. The sensation was familiar now, thrilling and yet soothing. With each of his swallows, her breathing slowed. Her limbs relaxed. Every nerve sang with delight. There was no striving for satisfaction. The truest and deepest pleasure was allowing herself to be consumed.

The sucking rhythm grew stronger. Dimly, through her trance, Lara understood that the vampire was fucking her as he drank. The sensations in her cunt became more acute, the pleasure sharp-edged rather than mellow. She felt every detail of his movements, how his cock pulsed as he wallowed in her sex. She felt him tear at her wrist, felt the blood flowing lazily down her forearm. He lapped at the overflow. The warmth of his tongue made her pussy clamp down on his hardness. Her clit was huge and sensitive. Each of his strokes produced electric arcs of pleasure that sizzled through her flesh.

Crimson clouds swirled around her. She smelled cinnamon and sulfur. Gradually, the more intense sensations faded. She did not miss them. The river was bearing her away, warm and wonderful. Her heart pumped sluggishly. She felt him, deep in her mind, sensed the way his terrible hunger receded as her life ebbed. She reached out to him, one last time, full of love and gratitude.

Agony suddenly replaced bliss, wrenching pain that filled the world. Seething blackness smothered her, roiling with horrible unseen forms. She couldn't breathe. Her throat was parched, her eyes stabbed by needles of anguish. Painful spasms wracked her limbs.

"Lara! Lara!" Someone was slapping her face, stinging blows that rattled her teeth in her head. "Come back, Lara!"

She gulped air and opened her eyes.

The room spun around her. Nausea rose in her throat, leaving an acid taste behind. Somehow she couldn't focus. Everything was blurry and the light seemed much too bright.

"Breathe, Lara. Focus. You're back... I'm sorry. I'm so sorry..."

Gradually the spinning stopped. The stabbing in her temples subsided to a dull ache, and her vision cleared.

Jim looked younger and more vulnerable than ever. He knelt next to the bed, holding her wrist in an iron grip, trying to staunch the blood that still dribbled from her torn flesh. He looked incredibly relieved when she managed to prop herself up to half-sitting.

"How do you feel?"

Lara interrogated her body. "Weak, and sore. But I guess I'm okay."

"I told you. I told you we wouldn't be able to stop."

"But we did. You did. I was ready to let it all go. But you're stronger than you realize." She looked him over. His face was flushed, and though his fangs were no longer visible, there were traces of blood at the corners of his mouth. "How do you feel? Better, I imagine, than before."

Jim frowned. "This isn't a joke, Lara! I almost killed you."

"So? Then I would have lived forever."

"Is that what you really want?" Lara remembered the terrible lust that she'd glimpsed in her vampire lover. She wasn't sure that she could endure that without going mad.

"I don't know. Maybe not. Maybe not—yet." He sat beside her on the bed. She reached out a finger and wiped the leftover blood from his lips. "But with you—well, let me just say that perhaps you don't need to be alone anymore."

"Are you crazy? I'm dangerous. I warned you."

"I'm willing to take risks." Lara reached out and began to stroke his still-hard cock. "At least when the payoff is worth it."

Jim moaned. Lara wondered briefly whether vampires could actually come. She vowed that she'd find out. "In any case, we're going to be seeing a lot of each other, now that you've joined the company."

"I don't know..."

"Look, I won't take any argument. I'll appoint you vice-president, let you make artistic decisions, whatever you want. But I must have you." She punctuated this with a squeeze that had Jim whimpering.

"Please..."

"Get over here. You haven't come yet, and just looking at you is turning me on."

Jim straddled her and slid his cock into her sore but sensitive pussy. After all the previous fucking, after paranormal ecstasy and a brush with death, he still felt delicious.

"And based on what I've learned from you, I know exactly what will be the next big thing for Vampires, Limited."

Jim moved inside her, slowly at first, then building up speed. He smiled down at her. "And just what would that be, Ms. Carter?"

Lara clamped down on him, coming hard. She couldn't talk until after the spasms subsided.

"Vampire sex clubs, of course!"

* * * *

Credits

"Jessebel" by Sacchi Green originally appeared in *Women of the Bite*, edited by Cecilia Tan (Alyson Books, 2009).

"Willing" by Xan West originally appeared in *Leathermen: Gay Erotic Stories*, edited by Simon Sheppard (Cleis Press, 2008)

"Kiss and Make Up" by Ashley Lister originally appeared in *The Sweetest Kiss: Ravishing Vampire Erotica,* edited by D.L. King (Cleis Press, 2009).

"Devouring Heart" by Andrea Dale originally appeared in *The Sweetest Kiss: Ravishing Vampire Erotica,* edited by D.L. King (Cleis Press, 2009).

"The Taste of B Negative" by Cheyenne Blue originally appeared in "Vamperotica"(Priveco Inc., 2012).

"Cat" by Giselle Renarde originally appeared (entitled "Blood Lust") in *Best Lesbian Erotica 2012*, edited by Kathleen Warnock and Sinclair Sexsmith (Cleis Press, 2011).

"Vampires, Limited" by Lisabet Sarai originally appeared in *Lust at First Bite: Sexy Vampire Short Stories* (Black Lace, 2008). We warmly thank Black Lace for permission to reprint in this volume

About the Contributors

NAOMI BELLINA lives in beautiful sunny Florida with the love of her life and a magical black cat. She writes for various fiction and non-fiction markets, but finds she is drawn to erotic romance because her characters insist on canoodling, and sometimes even falling madly in love. So she lets them. Occasionally, however, they go to dark and strange places. She lets them do this also. Most of her stories will surprise readers with unexpected twists and turns, because isn't that what makes life exciting?

Her interests include dancing, hula-hooping, drumming, and creating healthy meals. She takesthe opportunity to play, have fun, and indulge in the pursuit of passion whenever possible. She hopes you enjoy her stories and would love to hear from you at naomibellina(at)live(dot)com.

Visit her website at naomibellina.com

CHEYENNE BLUE's erotica has appeared in over 70 anthologies including *Best Women's Erotica, Mammoth Best New Erotica, Best Lesbian Erotica, Best Lesbian Romance, Girl Crazy, Cowboy Lust,* and *Girls Who Score.* She currently lives in Queensland, Australia, where the sunshine keeps away the dark creatures. Her preferred steaks are blue, her preferred wine is red, and her blood group is O negative. Visit her website at cheyenneblue.com.

Award winning author **KATHLEEN BRADEAN**'s stories can be found in *Carnal Machines, The Harder She Comes, Best of Best Women's Erotica* I and II, *Haunted Hearths* *and Sapphic Shades, The Sweetest Kiss: Vampire Tales,* and many other anthologies. She blogs for Oh Get A Grip, The Erotica Readers and Writer's Association, and reviews erotica at EroticaRevealed.com

M. CHRISTIAN is an acknowledged master of erotica with more than 300 stories in such anthologies as Best American Erotica, Best Gay Erotica, Best Lesbian Erotica, Best Bisexual Erotica, Best Fetish Erotica, and many, many other anthologies, magazines, and Web sites. He has edited twenty anthologies including the Best S/M Erotica series, The Burning Pen, Guilty Pleasures, and others, and the author of the collections *Dirty Words, Speaking Parts, The Bachelor Machine, Licks & Promises, Filthy, Love Without Gun Control, Rude Mechanicals,* and *Technorotica;* and the novels *Running Dry, The Very Bloody Marys, Me2, Brushes, Painted Doll,* and *Finger's Breadth.*

ANDREA DALE, a "legendary erotica heavy-hitter" (according to the über-legendary Violet Blue), writes sizzling erotica with a generous dash of romance. Her work—which has been called "poignantly erotic," "heartbreaking," and "exceptional"—has appeared in the Publisher's Weekly-starred Best Erotic Romance and Romantic Times 4-star anthology *Steamlust,* as well as about 100 other anthologies from Harlequin Spice, Avon Red, and Cleis Press. She finds passion in rock music, clever words, piercing blue eyes, the wind in her hair, and the scent of the ocean; and her favorite vampires are Spike and George Hamilton's Dracula (although Dracula's brides can be awfully hot, too). Under other names, she's a published author of fantasy, science fiction, media tie-in, and more. To find out where she's wandered off to or what her latest publications are, visit cyvarwydd.com.

Lisabet Sarai, editor

BERYL FALLS is a writer who lives in Sacramento, California. Her work has appeared in the Circlet Press Anthologies *Like Butterflies in Iron* and *Like a Coming Wave: Oceanic Erotica*. Over a decade ago Beryl was a passionate participant in poetry and short fiction workshops and began writing erotic stories six years ago. Now, by day she writes carefully crafted computer code, and by night creates erotic tales tailored for the individual, upon request. Her first screen crush was Bela Lugosi as Dracula, which led to a life-long love affair with the Vampire. She adores how the inherent eroticism of that creature allows the experience of merger, in all its subtle glory. She remains grateful that her two favorite subjects, sex, and the supernatural are currently enjoying such a fruitful union. In celebration of that, she has devoured as much of the film and literature devoted to that archetype as she can stomach, from *Vampyr* to *The Southern Vampire Mysteries*, pausing only to wipe her chin. A widow who lives alone in an 80 year old house, she also enjoys photography, reading horror and speculative fiction, dabbling in freeform crochet, and collecting and battling Beyblades.

SACCHI GREEN's stories have appeared in a hip-high stack of publications with erotically inspirational covers, including seven volumes of Best Lesbian Erotica, four of Best Lesbian Romance, three of The Mammoth Book of Best Erotica, and Penthouse. She's also edited or co-edited eight erotica anthologies, including *Girl Crazy*, *Lesbian Cowboys*, *Lesbian Lust*, *Lesbian Cops*, and *Girl Fever*, all from Cleis Press. Five of her books, including her collection *A Ride to Remember* from Lethe Press, have been finalists for the Lambda Literary Award, and *Lesbian Cowboys* was a winner.

Sacchi's alter-ego, Connie Wilkins, writes generally in the science fiction and fantasy genre, edited *Time Well Bent: Queer Alternative History*, and is co-editing *Heiresses of Russ 2012: the Year's Best Lesbian Speculative Fiction*, both for Lethe Press.

She lives and writes in both western Massachusetts and the mountains of New Hampshire, with frequent visits to the real world. Her online homes are Facebook (Sacchi Green) and sacchi-green.blogspot.com.

ASHLEY LISTER is a prolific writer of erotic fiction having written more than two dozen full length erotic novels and over a hundred short stories. Aside from regularly blogging about writing erotica, Ashley also teaches creative writing in the North West of England.

JAY LYGON swears each time he writes about vampires will be his last. That isn't working out well for him. Find his stories in *Blood Sacraments*, *Wings*, *Toy Box: Public Places*, and the *Bonded* series at Torquere Press. His trilogy of novels, *Chaos Magic*, *Love Runes,* and *Personal Demons* (Torquere Press) have been praised as "Magical realism, unlike any other BDSM novel ever written." Find Jay at JayLygonWrites.com.

RAZIEL MOORE started writing and sharing erotica last century, because he couldn't find the kind of stories that he wanted to read himself. So he made it. Over a decade later that remains one of his motivations. Sometimes ideas demand expression, putting characters - all shades of the writer, in the final analysis - in challenges and perils, or perpetrating the acts of monsters, human or otherwise. Moore believes that writing - and reading - frees us of the constraints of the civilized, moralized world. Our imaginations are unfettered. He can reach through this screen and take you, the reader, right now. Don't think he's not thinking about it. Right now. There's nothing you can do about it except close the page - or open your eyes and surrender. And if you're still reading, knowing the utterly obscene and awful things he's thinking of doing to you right now, well, that'll be your secret, won't it?

A few years ago **NOBILIS REED** decided to start sharing the naughty little stories he scribbled out in hidden notebooks. To his surprise, people actually liked them! Now, he can't stop. The poor man is addicted. His wife, teenage children, and even the cats just look on this wretch of a man, hunched over his computer and shake their heads. Clearly, there is no hope for him. The best thing to do is simply make him as comfortable as his condition will allow. Symptoms of his condition include two novels, several novellas, numerous short stories, and the longest-running erotica podcast in the history of the world. He has edited two anthologies for Coming Together: *In Flux* and *Arm in Arm in Arm...* Find his site at nobiliserotica.com, and his audio podcast at nobilis.libsyn.com.

Eroticist **GISELLE RENARDE** is a queer Canadian, avid volunteer, contributor to more than 50 short story anthologies, and author of dozens of electronic and print books. Some of her credits include 2011 Rainbow Awards Honourable Mention *My Mistress' Thighs: Erotic Transgender Fiction and Poetry*, *The Red Satin Collection* (loveyoudivine Alterotica), *Anonymous* (Amber Allure),

Ondine (Hudson Audiobooks/eXcessica Publishing), and *Audrey & Lawrence* (eXcessica Publishing). Ms Renarde lives across from a park with two bilingual cats who sleep on her head. Visit Giselle at wix.com/gisellerenarde/erotica

At this particular time in a wandering, often bizarre and unexpected life, **C. SANCHEZ-GARCIA** is living quietly in eastern Georgia, where the size of his personal library is bursting the walls of his little house. He stubbornly believes in passion, God, sensuality and spirituality, and that a good love story is life's finest medicine for melancholy. He is the author of the erotic novellas *Mortal Engines and the Color of the Moon.* His stories have been published in the *Mammoth Book of Best New Erotica* and Coming Together anthologies, as well as in his single-author charitable collection, Coming Together Presents C. Sanchez-Garcia. If you would like to meet the author you will find him on Facebook and at the Erotica Readers & Writers Association blog (erotica-readers.blogspot.com).

More than a dozen years ago, **LISABET SARAI** experienced a serendipitous fusion of her love of writing and her fascination with sex. Since then, she has published seven erotic novels, including the BDSM classic *Raw Silk,* and five short story collections, as well as many shorter works. Her stories have appeared in dozens of print and ebook collections edited by such erotica luminaries as M. Christian, Maxim Jakubowski, Mitzi Szereto, Rachel Kramer Bussel, Alison Tyler, and Alessia Brio (including many Coming Together anthologies).

Lisabet co-edited the ground-breaking anthology *Sacred Exchange* (Blue Moon Books, 2003), which explores the spiritual aspects of BDSM relationships, and edited

Lisabet Sarai, editor

Cream: The Best of the Erotica Readers and Writers Association (Running Press, 2006). She also works as a free-lance editor and reviews books and films for the Erotica Readers and Writers Association and Erotica Revealed.

Lisabet holds a PhD and two Masters degrees from prestigious universities that might well be embarrassed to acknowledge her erotic writing career. Visit her site, Lisabet's Fantasy Factory (lisabetsarai.com) and her blog Beyond Romance (lisabetsarai.blogspot.com).

KIMBER VALE is an avid reader, writer, and gardener. She worked as an RN in a previous life. Currently, she raises three small people and puts fantasies to computer screen in her spare time. She writes both gay and straight erotica, as well as bizarro, and prefers stories with dark and delicious undertones. Check out her hetero story in "Cowboy Lust" from Cleis Press, and her M/M novelette "Bound by Ink" in Storm Moon Press' *Written in Ink* tattoo-themed anthology. Kimber additionally pens horror stories without the sexy stuff using the name on her driver's license. Stop by her salacious blog for info and insolence at kimbervale.wordpress.com. Find her on Facebook and Twitter @KimberVale.

XAN WEST is the nom de plume of a Brooklyn based queer BDSM/sex educator and writer. It's been said that "if you like your BDSM on the brutal side, you can always count on Xan West to deliver.", and that Xan's work "ought to come with a warning for the faint-hearted". Xan's story "First Time Since", won honorable mention for the 2008 National Leather Association John Preston Short Fiction Award. Xan's sci fi/fantasy work is printed in *SexTime: Erotic Stories of Time Travel, Leathermen,*

Men at Noon, Monsters at Midnight, Blood Sacraments, and *Wired Hard 4.* Xan's gay erotica appears in numerous anthologies, including *Coming Together: In Flux, Best Gay Erotica 2009, Daddies, Hot Daddies, Hurts So Good, Love at First Sting, Bondage by the Bay, Biker Boys, Brief Encounters, Backdraft: Firemen Erotica, Men on the Edge, I Like to Watch,* and *In Plain View.* Xan wants to hear from you Xan_West@yahoo.com.

* * * *

Lisabet Sarai, editor

About Coming Together

Coming Together is about giving and about sex—a tantalizing combination in any context. Conceived online in the Literotica®com Authors' Hangout, a forum for erotica writers, Coming Together is the passionate product of many talented individuals.

We were all amateurs when the first erotic cocktail was served in the spring of 2005. In the years since the inaugural volume hit the cyber shelves of Café Press, many of the original contributors have become successful professionals: authors, poets, editors, and artists. To date, Coming Together has compiled over a dozen collections, launched individual full-length and novella lines, and has many more anthologies in the works. I am thrilled with and humbled by both the quantity and quality of the submissions received.

In each volume, we strive for an inclusive mix, embracing the diversity of desire. The causes we champion cross all demographic groups and so, appropriately, does Coming Together. Note, however, that these pages may contain fantastic stories in which the characters do not practice safe sex. Everyone involved with the publication of Coming Together encourages its readers to act responsibly and to take appropriate precautions against both unwanted pregnancy and the transmission of disease.

Bottoms up!

peace & passion,

Alessia Brio

purpleprosaic.com